D0323989

GRAVEBOOKS

J. A. White

GRAVEBOOKS

THE SEQUEL TO
NIGHTBOOKS

 KATHERINE TEGEN BOOKS
An Imprint of HarperCollinsPublishers

Katherine Tegen Books is an imprint of HarperCollins Publishers.

Gravebooks

Copyright © 2022 by J. A. White
All rights reserved. Printed in the United States of America.
No part of this book may be used or reproduced in any manner whatsoever without
written permission except in the case of brief quotations embodied in critical articles
and reviews. For information address HarperCollins Children's Books, a division of
HarperCollins Publishers, 195 Broadway, New York, NY 10007.
www.harpercollinschildrens.com

ISBN 978-0-06-308201-4

Typography by Amy Ryan
22 23 24 25 26 PC/LSCH 10 9 8 7 6 5 4 3 2 1
❖
First Edition

When I was a boy, the following authors inspired me
to write my own creepy tales:

Robert Bloch
Ray Bradbury
Shirley Jackson
Stephen King
Richard Matheson

This book is dedicated to them.
Thanks for the nightmares!

CONTENTS

NIGHTBOOKS

There was once a boy named Alex who liked to write scary stories. He was kidnapped by a witch and held captive in her magic apartment. The witch's name was Natacha, and her cruelty knew no bounds. She told Alex he had to do her bidding. If not, she would turn him into a porcelain figurine, just like the other children she had trapped over the years. Fortunately, Natacha liked scary stories. As long as he read her a new one each night, she would let him live.

This might have been the end of Alex's tale, were it not for a girl and a cat. The girl's name was Yasmin. She had been held captive much longer than Alex. Her job was making the magic oils that Natacha sold throughout the kingdom of New York City. The cat's name was Lenore, and she was the witch's familiar. These three didn't get along at first, but after a few misadventures they became friends and decided to escape.

They soon discovered that Natacha had been stealing her powers from a fairy-tale witch who she kept trapped in a magically induced slumber. The true witch woke up, ate the false witch, and nearly did away with Alex and Yasmin as well. Fortunately, they were able to get the best of her in the end, and the spell was lifted from all the kids who had been transformed into porcelain figurines.

A year passed. Alex and Yasmin returned to their normal lives. They thought they were done with witches.

They were wrong.

I

THE PAINTED MOON

Alex Mosher found himself standing in a graveyard.

Normally he wouldn't have minded. He liked grave-yards. There were only two problems. First, it was nighttime. Crypts and tombstones possessed an odd sort of beauty when the sun was in the sky, but at night they were simply scary.

The second problem was even worse.

Alex had no idea how he had gotten there.

Hoping to spark his memory, he started to explore. It was a strange graveyard. There were no paths of any kind, no orderly rows of tombstones. As far as Alex could tell, the graves had been dug at random. Some were far apart, others practically touching. A neat rectangle of black soil sat in front of each tombstone.

All the graves were fresh.

Alex closed his eyes and tried to retrace the steps that had led him there. The last thing he remembered was sitting at his bedroom desk and working on a new story. It hadn't been going well, which was pretty much the norm these days. Alex had wanted to write a werewolf story, but he couldn't come up with a fresh take. A kid werewolf? Boring. A werewolf that gets bitten by a vampire? Alex was pretty sure that had been done before. His final idea of the night had been a story about a detective searching for a missing werewolf. He was going to call it "Wherewolf."

At that point, Alex had known it was time to go to bed.

But what happened after that?

"I read for a little while," he said, picturing himself propped up against a pillow with his battered copy of *Something Wicked This Way Comes.* "Will and Jim had just met Mr. Dark."

It was Alex's fourth time reading Ray Bradbury's famous novel about a dark carnival. He barely remembered his first journey through the book, a fever dream that had ended only when he turned the last page and noticed that night had become day. His subsequent readings had been slower as he tried to decipher how Mr. Bradbury had made his words dance and sing. No matter how many times Alex reread passages or copied them by hand, however, their power remained a magician's secret far beyond his ability to comprehend.

"I underlined a phrase I liked," Alex said. "'Yet here he stood, moon-calm, inhabiting his itchweed suit.'" Speaking the words out loud filled him with wonder at their beauty but also a kind of despair; no matter how many stories he wrote, he'd never be *that* good. "Then I put the book on my bedside table and went to sleep. . . ."

Was he *dreaming*?

It didn't seem possible. Alex took a deep breath and felt his lungs expand, then rubbed cool blades of grass between his fingertips. This was real. It had to be. On the other hand, why wasn't he cold? It was late spring, and while the days were finally beginning to warm up, the nights refused to relinquish their chilly hold. Yet here he was in jeans and a T-shirt, totally comfortable. There was also, he now noticed, no breeze at all. The wind was as dead as the corpses underfoot.

Still, Alex struggled to believe this was all a dream. Maybe it was just an unusually mild night.

It was the moon that finally convinced him. Not only was it bigger and lower than usual, but there was something oddly flat about its appearance. It reminded Alex of certain old horror movies where even the outdoor scenes had been filmed indoors, and the sky was nothing but a painted backdrop.

That's not the real moon, he thought. *This* is *a dream!*

Alex felt a little better. Nothing could hurt you in a dream. This was just his crazy imagination at work, and at some point, he'd wake up. Now more curious than afraid, he decided to learn as much as possible about the graveyard. The first question that popped into his mind was an obvious one: Who was buried here? By the light of the false moon, he examined the nearest gravestone. There was no name, no dates, no epitaph. Instead, a wire cage, like something you might use to house a small animal, had been engraved into the stone.

"Maybe this is a pet cemetery," Alex said. He moved on to the next tombstone, expecting to see an engraving of a leash or maybe some paw prints.

It was a picnic basket.

"Huh," said Alex, totally bewildered now. A cage made sense—sort of—but a picnic basket? What was going on here? Alex's confusion only grew as he continued his investigation. In no time at all, he had found an engraving of a mailbox, a stethoscope, an old-fashioned key, a necklace, and a cave. The engravings were strange but also maddeningly familiar.

"What kind of graveyard is this?" Alex asked, tracing the swirls of a giant lollipop with his finger. Since there was no name or date, did the lollipop somehow relate to the person buried there? "Maybe it's a kid with a sweet tooth," Alex said. He gasped as a second, darker thought occurred to him: What if the lollipop represented the cause of death? The kid could have been poisoned—or choked to death.

Maybe each engraving revealed the way the person buried there had died.

"Cool!" said Alex.

He practically skipped around the cemetery, eager to test his theory. A few engravings were slam dunks—dagger, car, spiderweb—but most were a stretch at best. How did someone get killed by a postage stamp? Or a cloud? Or an asterisk?

"Guess it must be something else," Alex said, baffled.

He heard a high-pitched howl and saw a black animal with tall, pointed ears and gray eyes. Some people might have mistaken it for a dog, but Alex had written two stories based on Egyptian mythology and knew a jackal when he saw one. It bared its teeth and sauntered in his direction. Alex backed away, keeping his eyes on the animal. It seemed pointless to run. The jackal was much faster than him, and there was nowhere to hide.

"It's okay," Alex said to himself. "It's only a dream. Nothing here can hurt you."

He backed straight into a warm body. Before he could

turn around, a familiar voice whispered, "Hey there, story-teller."

Alex gasped. This wasn't a dream. It was a nightmare.

Natacha was back.

2

A GRAVE REUNION

The former resident of apartment 4E looked exactly the same: short black hair, a thick layer of makeup, and an overall fashion sense that could best be described as "aggressively witchy."

"Impossible," Alex croaked.

"They said the same thing about sending a man to the moon. Everything's impossible until it's not anymore."

"The Candy Witch gobbled you up. You're dead!"

"Oh, Alex. Haven't you learned a single thing from all those horror stories? Witches don't die. They *evolve*." Natacha looked him over with an appraising expression, like a distant relative who hadn't seen him in years. "You're taller. I don't like it. I prefer you small and defenseless."

"This is just a dream. You can't hurt me."

"Well, you're right about the dream part," Natacha said.

The jackal took a seat by her side. "This is Simeon, by the way. My new familiar. A vast improvement over Lenore. How is the traitorous feline, anyway?"

"All I have to do is wake up and you'll be gone," Alex said.

"That easy, huh? All right, then. Show me what you've got." She looked down at Simeon and added, "This kid escaped one magical apartment and now he thinks he's Houdini."

Alex closed his eyes and willed himself back to his warm bed. When that didn't work, he took a fold of skin between his fingers and squeezed it as hard as he could. The pain felt real enough, but when Alex opened his eyes, he remained trapped in the dream. He tried pinching a few other spots, just in case.

Natacha asked, "What exactly is the game plan here?"

"I read once that if you pinch yourself in a dream, you'll wake up in real life."

"I read that little boys taste best with a dash of cilantro. We read very different books, don't we?"

Alex pinched himself one last time and gave up.

"This can't be happening!" he exclaimed. "You're not her! You're just a figment of my imagination!"

"Believe what you want," replied Natacha. She snapped her fingers and a shovel appeared in Alex's hand. "In the meantime, start digging. It doesn't matter where. Any grave will do."

Alex stared at the shovel in disbelief. The rough handle promised splinters, and the blade was orange with rust.

"You want me to dig up a dead body?" he asked.

"I want you to dig up a dead *idea*."

"Huh?"

"Haven't you figured it out yet?" She poked him in the forehead. "So many ideas are born in that weird little brain of yours. Some of them become stories. But the ones you don't use? They just wither and die. This graveyard is where they're buried."

Alex instantly knew that Natacha was telling the truth. The idea of a story graveyard somehow felt *right*. He supposed he had already known on one level or another. This was his mind, after all.

"Some ideas are pretty far along," Natacha continued. "Maybe you made an outline or wrote a few pages. You brought them to life, at least for a day or two. And then you gave up. Seems like that's been happening a lot lately. Strange. You never had trouble finishing stories back in the apartment. What happened?"

"Nothing," Alex said, feeling his cheeks grow warm. "Everything's fine."

"Uh-huh. Now, some of these other ideas are little

more than whispers. A thought you had on the school bus one day and forgot by the time the first bell rang." She jabbed him in the chest, as though Alex's inability to finish every story was some kind of personal affront. "Such a waste of precious imagination! Honestly, you should be ashamed of yourself."

Alex's fear took a momentary back seat to his curiosity. "Do the engravings represent the idea, then? Like, that one right there with the web—is it a story about some kind of spider?"

"More than likely. Sometimes the engravings aren't so on the nose, though. It might not be about a spider at all. It could be . . . I don't know . . ."

"Metaphorical. Like a web of deceit."

Natacha looked impressed—and a little cautious. "I've forgotten how quick you are. Listen, we can guess what *might* be buried here all day long, but wouldn't it be more fun to dig it up and find out for sure? Frankly, you owe it to these guys. Poor little ideas! All they ever wanted to do was grow up and become stories, and you let them die!"

Strange as it seemed, Alex felt a little guilty. "I didn't do it on purpose," he stammered. "I just couldn't figure them out."

"Well, good news, storyteller! This is your chance to make up for it. Just dig up an idea—any idea—and write the story!"

It was tempting. He was dying to know what lay beneath each grave, and this was just a dream, after all. But Alex's sense of survival, sharpened to a keen edge during his time in the apartment, was warning him that things were more dangerous than they seemed.

She's here for a reason. You dig up that grave, and you're doing exactly what she wants. That can't be good.

"No," Alex said.

Simeon raised his head and snarled. His teeth looked very real. Alex tried to remember that he was in his bed right now, safe and sound. It wasn't easy.

"Color me perplexed," Natacha said, tapping her long black nails against the top of the tombstone. "You love to write! And this time, you're not trapped in an apartment with that annoying girl. You can write at night from the safety of your bed and go about your business during the day. Honestly, you should be thanking me for the opportunity!"

"The Candy Witch is dead. There's no more magic for you to steal. So why do you still want my stories?"

Natacha offered an innocent shrug. "Because I love them, Alex. I'm your biggest fan."

Alex's ego wanted to believe her, but he knew it couldn't be that simple. Nothing with Natacha ever was.

He tossed the shovel away.

"I'm not doing this," Alex said. "And you can't make me."

13

Natacha exchanged a knowing look with Simeon.

"I told you he's a stubborn one. But don't worry. He'll come around. Soon enough, he'll be writing us a new story every night."

"I'm not writing you a single sentence ever again! Now get out of my dream!"

Natacha raised her hands in defeat. "Okay, storyteller. I had to try."

She vanished into thin air, taking her familiar with her. Instead of being relieved by Natacha's absence, Alex felt more wary than ever. "That was way too easy," he mumbled. He scanned the horizon in every direction, expecting to see the witch watching him from afar. All he saw were gravestones and a few scattered trees.

She was really gone—for now, at least.

"If she was even here at all," Alex said. More than likely, he had simply imagined her—though it was a little weird that he had also created a new familiar to keep her company. Then again, his imagination *was* weird. Alex couldn't always explain the choices it made.

He decided to keep exploring. Alex wasn't planning to dig up any graves, but he picked up the shovel and propped it over his shoulder anyway—he felt better having something he could use as a weapon, just in case Natacha had any other tricks up her sleeve. Hopefully he would wake up soon. Alex had already been in the graveyard for what felt like hours, so it was only a matter of time before he was rescued by the morning sun. He trekked past gravestones and obelisks and the occasional crypt, pausing every so often to check out an engraving. Finally, it began to rain. Alex looked up at the darkening sky and saw the moon dissolving into smears of silver light that lost their luster as they hit the ground. Within moments, the world was plunged into darkness. Alex stood perfectly still, afraid to move. He could hear scratching noises in the graves around him, as though creatures who might have been kept at bay by the light of the moon were now beginning to crawl to the surface.

And then it was daytime.

The sun didn't rise; it simply appeared. Like the moon, it looked as though it had been painted onto the sky. Its light was the sickly yellow of a hospital waiting room.

Hoping for a better vantage point, Alex climbed to the top of a hill. From here, he could see for miles in every direction. The graveyard went on forever. Alex felt like an astronaut who had crash-landed on a planet of the dead. *That's not a bad idea for a story*, he thought, and wondered if a rocket ship was being engraved into a tombstone somewhere.

"I have to wake up eventually, don't I?" Alex asked.

He wasn't so sure anymore.

After walking a bit farther, he noticed something odd.

Although the ground seemed to be moving beneath his feet, the tombstones in front of him weren't getting any closer, and the spindly oak tree to his left wasn't getting any farther away. It was as though the grass was a treadmill in disguise, giving him only the feeling of movement while keeping him in place. Alex tested a few more spots and got the same results; although there wasn't a physical fence, he was pretty sure he had reached the end of the graveyard.

He turned around and headed back the way he had come.

At the end of the day, a new storm washed away the sun, and the painted moon reappeared in the sky. Alex was beginning to panic. He wasn't cold. He wasn't hungry. He wasn't anything. *Now I know what a ghost feels like*, he thought with a shiver. Alex could imagine the days stretching into years with nothing but these tombstones to keep him company.

There was only one thing he hadn't tried yet: digging up an idea and writing a story. In fact, Alex was starting to wonder if that was the only way to escape the graveyard at all.

"Don't give in," Alex said. He had been talking to himself so much that it no longer felt strange. "That's what Natacha wants."

Night became day. Alex began to recognize some of

the engravings. He assumed he had retraced his path, although he was too disoriented to tell anymore. Finally, he reached the engraving of the pet cage and knew that he had circled all the way back to the beginning. Alex sat against the tombstone and cradled his face in his hands.

Sometime later, he felt something soft and warm brush against his arm. Alex screamed and scrambled away. This initial shock, however, was quickly replaced by joy as he saw the identity of this unexpected visitor.

"Lenore!" he exclaimed.

Alex threw his arms around the orange cat and held her tight. She felt blissfully warm and real. Lenore wasn't much of a hugger, however, so it wasn't long before she slipped out of his arms and took a seat on the grass.

"How did you get here?" Alex asked.

Lenore looked insulted. She was hundreds of years old, had retractable fingers instead of claws, and could turn herself invisible at will. Why *wouldn't* she be able to enter his dreams?

"It doesn't matter," Alex said. "I'm just glad you're here."

Lenore nodded: *You should be.* She did a quick scan of the graveyard and fixed him with expectant green eyes, waiting for an explanation. Alex started from the beginning. Lenore hissed when he mentioned Natacha's name but otherwise remained silent.

When Alex was done, Lenore picked up a handful of

grave dirt with her tiny fingers and flung it onto the grass.

"You think I should dig?" Alex asked.

Lenore tossed a second handful of dirt at Alex's chest. She got testy when she had to repeat herself.

"I'm willing to try anything at this point, but are you sure that's a good idea? I feel like we're playing right into Natacha's hands."

Lenore's question-mark tail waved up and down, which was her version of a shrug: *What choice do you have?*

"So you're saying if I don't do this, Rusty and I will be stuck here forever?"

Lenore tilted her head to one side: *Rusty?*

"That's what I named my shovel! Which, now that I'm saying it out loud, sounds a little bananas. Have I mentioned that I've been in this graveyard for a really long time?"

Lenore gave him a pitying look—as though he might possibly be beyond her help—and hopped onto the tombstone to watch him dig. Alex thrust the blade of the shovel into the dirt and started a pile to the side of the grave. The earth was loose and moved easily. Before long, he struck something solid. With a combination of fear and excitement, Alex began to dig faster, eventually unearthing a plain pine box.

A coffin.

"I don't get it," Alex said, hopping out of the grave.

Standing on the coffin—and, more importantly, what might be *inside* the coffin—was making him nervous. "Natacha said there weren't any actual bodies buried in this graveyard."

From her perch atop the tombstone, Lenore pointed to the coffin with the tip of her tail: *Only one way to find out.*

"I don't know, Lenore. Bad things happen when you open coffins in graveyards. You don't have to be a horror movie buff to know that one."

Lenore leaped onto the coffin, moving with a preternatural grace that belied her size, and thumped the lid three times with her tail.

"Okay," Alex said. "I hope you know what you're doing." He jammed the blade of the shovel beneath the lid and pushed down on the handle. There was a loud crack, and the lid came loose.

A slate-gray notebook materialized on top of the tombstone.

Alex picked it up. "Guess this is where Natacha expects me to write my story," he said. The book was heavier than he expected and had a familiar picture on the cover. "Look, Lenore! It's the same cage as the one on the tombstone. The grave and the book must be connected somehow. I guess that makes this a . . . gravebook. Get it?"

Lenore looked unamused.

Alex returned to the coffin and dug his fingers beneath

the lid. It was a flimsy piece of wood, and he was able to lift it with ease.

He looked down.

The coffin had no bottom. Instead, Alex was able to look *through* the coffin to some kind of warehouse. Three-tiered metal shelves stretched down a wide aisle. The shelves were packed with what Alex assumed were boxes or crates, though there was no way to know for sure. Each of them was covered with a thick black sheet.

"Whoa," Alex said, falling to his knees. He felt dizzy. Since he was looking down through the opening, the logical side of his brain assumed he should have a bird's-eye view of the warehouse. Instead, his perspective was that of a person standing on the floor.

He leaned over the edge of the hole and stretched his arm through the coffin's doorway.

There was no resistance, no tingling, no pain. It was no different than reaching through an open window. Alex could see his hand in the warehouse and feel the cold tile floor. He felt a small, hard object pass beneath his fingertips and brought it through the opening. It was a brown pellet, like something you might feed a guinea pig. Lenore took a quick sniff and grimaced in disgust. She found the concept of pet food morally offensive.

"What do you think, Lenore?" Alex asked. "Should we check it out?"

With no hesitation whatsoever, Lenore leaped through the opening and stared back at Alex from the warehouse floor. There was a playful look in her eyes, as though she was daring him to follow her.

Refusing to be outdone by a magical cat, Alex clasped the gravebook tight and dropped through the coffin.

3

ANYTHING BUT DOGS!

Passing through the coffin was a disorienting experience. At first, Alex felt like he was falling, then the world seemed to tilt upward and catch him with solid ground. He tottered unsteadily for a moment. When the dizziness had finally passed, he took stock of his new surroundings.

He was standing in the aisle of black-cloaked shapes.

Gentle piano music, like something you might hear at the mall, piped through the speakers. The coffin stood directly behind him. It was taller than Alex and looked out of place beneath the fluorescent lights, like a Halloween decoration at a wedding. Looking through it, he saw the painted moon in the sky.

Alex realized this wasn't a warehouse, as he had initially suspected, but one of those huge megastores, like Walmart or Costco. From here he could see a dozen checkout lanes, currently empty, and a long train of shopping carts awaiting use. There weren't any doors or windows.

A blue banner hanging from the ceiling read ANYTHING BUT DOGS!

"This dream keeps getting weirder and weirder," Alex said. Lenore gave one of her rare meows in agreement.

Alex didn't see any customers roaming the aisles, but there was a wax figure of a teenage boy perched on a stool behind one of the cash registers. He was wearing a pink polo shirt embroidered with a crossed-out dog.

"Awesome," said Alex, leaning over the counter for a closer look at the wax figure. "Check out the details on this thing."

Lenore, clearly less enthused than her human companion, hopped onto the counter and gave the teenager a hesitant poke with her tail. The touch, however slight, seemed to activate something. Machinery clanked and popped behind the cashier's chest. A moment later, he started to speak, the words issuing from a speaker buried behind his motionless lips. His stiff arms gestured toward the aisles like an old-fashioned animatronic.

"Thank you for shopping at Anything but Dogs! We are here to help you with all your pet needs! Unless you want a dog, ha ha!" His voice grew disturbingly serious.

"We don't sell those and never will."

Lenore nodded, as though she heartily approved of this business model.

"Do you work here?" Alex asked.

"That's right! I'm here to help."

"What's your name?"

The wax figure remained silent. Alex noticed that his name tag was blank. *Because I never named him*, Alex thought with a twinge of guilt. *He's just a side character.*

"Are we still in the graveyard, or is this somewhere else?" Alex asked.

Silence.

"Do you know what Natacha wants?"

Silence.

"What's two plus two?"

Silence.

Alex sighed. The cashier clearly had a very limited set of knowledge. It was pointless to grill him for information outside his area of expertise. Besides, right now Alex's priority was waking up as quickly as possible. The amount of time he'd spent in the dream was beginning to frighten him.

"Do you have any pets that might make a good story?" Alex asked.

"All the pets at Anything but Dogs! are stories just

waiting to happen," the wax figure replied. "Do you have a particular genre in mind?"

"Horror."

"Try aisle three."

"Thanks," Alex said. He took a few steps away and then turned back. "I have to know. Why don't you sell dogs?"

The cashier looked confused. "That was your only rule when you created this place. Anything but dogs!"

"Got it!" Alex exclaimed, finally understanding. As they searched the store for aisle three, he walked Lenore through his epiphany. "A few months ago, I decided to write a scary pet story. I had no idea if I was going to write about a fake animal or a make-believe one, or what was going to happen. In fact, there was only one thing I knew for sure—the pet wouldn't be a dog. I'd already written a dog story back in the apartment, and I wanted to do something different. I scribbled down a bunch of ideas, but none of them took, so I eventually just forgot about it." Alex looked around the store in wonder. "Except I guess I didn't *totally* forget about it. The idea just got buried and became . . . this."

They found aisle three, which looked identical to all the other aisles: long shelves, rectangular shapes draped in black. Alex approached the nearest one and removed the cover, revealing a metal cage lined with torn newspaper.

Two mice—one brown, one white—cowered in the corner, frightened by the sudden light.

Alex held up the gravebook and compared the cage on the cover to the one in front of him. It was a perfect match. "Guess we know where the engraving on the tombstone comes from," he said.

Lenore inched closer to the cage, eyeing the mice with keen interest. She might have been a magical creature who had lived for hundreds of years, but she was still a cat.

"Don't even think about it," Alex said. "They're so cute!"

The brown mouse opened its mouth and a long tongue, like that of a frog, shot out and wrapped itself around Lenore's paw. She tried to scramble away, but the tongue was stronger than it looked and held her in place. While the brown mouse took a few steps back, strengthening its position like a cowboy lassoing a bull, the white mouse began to tightrope across the tongue on its hind legs, pausing at the edge of the cage to pluck out one of its whiskers. It looked as sharp as a needle.

The white mouse reached back with its tiny paw, ready to sling the whisker like a javelin at Lenore's eye.

"Hey!" Alex screamed, smacking the cage. The white mouse toppled from its perch, and the brown mouse tumbled head over paws as its tongue snapped into place. The mice looked up at their attacker with angry little faces, the white one already withdrawing a second whisker.

Alex quickly covered the cage.

"Maybe they're not so cute after all," Alex said. "Let's keep looking."

They continued down the aisle, pausing to investigate each cage. Some animals were perfectly normal. Others . . . not so much. Alex saw fur with too many eyes and eyes with too much fur; shy ooze peeking out of an overturned coffee cup; a bespectacled bat that spoke in ancient Greek; eggs of various shapes, sizes, and colors; a backpack with tentacles instead of straps; spider monkeys; monkey spiders; a smug-looking rabbit wearing a tortoise shell; and a goat with the face of Alex's least favorite teacher.

The aisle went on forever. Alex recognized some of the animals from a list he had made while brainstorming ideas for the story. The rest were a mystery. Either he had forgotten them altogether, or they had been born somewhere in his subconscious while he wasn't paying attention. If this dream was proof of one thing, it was that Alex's imagination was constantly at work, even when he wasn't aware of it.

He returned to the front of the store. The nameless cashier gave him a stiff-armed wave.

"Did you find what you were looking for?" he asked.

"I'm not sure yet," Alex replied.

He found a spot behind the register of an unoccupied checkout lane and placed the gravebook on the counter.

"Here goes nothing," he muttered. Alex opened the book, and a black pen with a sharp metallic tip rolled out. He tested it by scrawling his name on the first page. The letters appeared in a series of jagged cuts, as though he had carved them into a tree.

"How's this going to work, Lenore?" he asked, tapping the pen on the counter. "This story is supposed to be about a pet, but no one would want one of those weird animals in their house. So how does the main character get it? Bad birthday present? Curse? It follows him home?"

Lenore yawned.

"Yeah, you're right. Too complicated. Maybe it would be better to use a pet that starts out normal and gets weird later on. This way I can get right to the good stuff without explaining anything. But what animal should I use?"

Lenore puffed out her chest.

"Sorry, buddy. There are already so many cat stories. I want to do something more creative than that." He let out a long sigh. "I don't know. Maybe I *should* use one of the animals here."

Lenore covered her face with a paw.

"Let me think about this . . ."

Alex made a list of the strangest animals he had seen in the pet store, hoping to feature one of them in his story. No matter how hard he tried, however, he couldn't fashion a plot strong enough to cage the wild creations. His imagination simply wasn't up to the task.

"I'll just stick to a regular animal, then," he said, disappointed in himself. Resorting to a real-world pet felt like giving up. "I need to write *something* so I can get out of here. It doesn't need to be a masterpiece."

Alex pieced together a simple plot. It wasn't the most original story in the world, but at least it worked. Right now, that was the best he could do. He smoothed down the first page of the gravebook and took a deep breath. Writing used to come so easily to him. During the past year, however, a tiny voice had taken residence in his head and begun to question every decision he made. As Alex wrote the first sentence, he could already hear its nasally whispers: *Are you sure this is where you want to start the story? Is that the right word? Will anyone actually want to read this?* Alex tuned out the voice as best he could and climbed uphill through one page, then another, then another after that.

At last, he finished.

Alex wasn't exactly happy with the end result. If he had been sitting in the comfort of his home, he would have exiled the story to his lower desk drawer, where it could gather dust with his growing pile of unfinished drafts. He didn't have that luxury right now, however, so he supposed it would have to do. Hopefully it was good enough to satisfy Natacha and get him back to the real world.

Alex closed the gravebook.

It burst into flames.

"Ahh!" he screamed, leaping off his stool and studying the silver-tinted blaze from a safe distance. The flames weren't spreading. In fact, they seemed incapable of touching anything other than the gravebook, which they reduced to ashes in no time at all.

Tears welled in Alex's eyes.

"All that work for nothing!" he exclaimed. "That was a really good story, too!" (Now that it was gone, Alex's opinion of his work had improved, in the same way one might think more highly of a person after his untimely demise.) "Is Natacha messing with me? Or did she somehow read the story and think it wasn't good enough?" He buried his face in Lenore's fur. "What are we going to do now?"

The entire store began to shake, rattling cages and knocking shelves to the ground. The animals, which until this point had remained relatively quiet, exploded into a chorus of shrieks, growls, roars, yips, and a few other sounds that Alex didn't recognize. He heard a loud thud and saw that the wax cashier had tipped over on his stool. His name tag popped loose from his shirt and clattered across the floor.

"Don't be afraid," the cashier said, his voice garbled and broken. He got stuck on the last word—*afraidafraid afraid*—before the gears that ran his life engine finally came to a merciful halt.

With Lenore in the lead, Alex fled toward the grave-yard. A wailing wind battered him from side to side; the floor bucked beneath his feet. At last, he reached the cof-fin. During his time in the pet store, the false sun had risen in the sky and cast a rectangle of blinding light across the floor. Shielding his eyes, Alex leaped through the open-ing. He was in the graveyard for just a moment, hanging in midair with the sky overhead, before finding himself lying on the floor of the pet store. Alex sprang to his feet, instantly realizing his mistake. *It looks like I'm going for-ward from this direction*, he thought. *But I actually have to climb up through the grave.* With no time to lose, Alex leaped through the opening and caught the upper edge of the coffin on the graveyard side. From here, he dug his hands into the dirt and clawed his way to the surface.

Natacha was waiting for him with crossed arms, reminding Alex of his mother whenever he returned late from a friend's house. If he hadn't been so terrified, he might have laughed.

"Took you long enough!" Natacha screamed over the cataclysmic noises issuing from the grave world below them. It sounded like an on-the-scene news report about a category five hurricane.

"What's happening?" Alex asked, looking down at the pet store. Dozens of cages, their black covers lost to the wind, were flying through the air. Strange animals stared at Alex as they vanished out of view, as though he was to blame.

"You finished your story!" Natacha exclaimed. "You don't need that idea anymore, so your mind is taking out the trash!"

She tossed the lid back on the coffin, creating some kind of aural seal that instantly cut off the sounds of the pet store. The graveyard seemed quieter than ever.

"I finished the story, sure," Alex said with slumped shoulders, "but then the gravebook burst into flames. It's gone."

Natacha huffed in annoyance. "You really don't know anything, do you?"

She spun Alex around until he was facing the tombstone, which had grown even taller than Natacha. The engraving of the cage had been replaced by hundreds of tiny words etched carefully into the stone. They were in Alex's handwriting. At the top of the tombstone was a single word centered against the rest of the text:

NIBBLES

"My story!" Alex exclaimed. "But how? I watched it burn up."

"Those were flames of transference, not destruction.

The book and the gravestone are connected. When you finished your story, it simply moved to its new home."

With a look of wonder, Alex trailed his fingertips over his rescued tale. "That's why it felt like I was scratching the words into the page, not writing them. They were coming here. I call it a gravebook, by the way."

"Adorable," replied Natacha. "Now shut up and let me read."

NIBBLES

Jude heard the scratching again.

He sat up in bed, hoping it had just been a nightmare. But even after wiping the sleep from his eyes, Jude could still hear it, a whisper of nails against cardboard. He tossed the covers aside and looked out his bedroom window at a small mound of dirt in the backyard garden. It was where he had buried his guinea pig, Nibbles, three days ago.

The scratching was coming from her grave.

"It's just my imagination," Jude said, shaking his head. "The stupid fur ball's dead."

Jude had never wanted a pet. The whole guinea pig experiment had been a misguided attempt by his mom to teach him "responsibility." If Nibbles had gotten sick because he rarely fed her and only cleaned her cage when his mom complained about the stench, whose fault was that? His mother's, clearly.

Scritchscratch. Scritchscratch.

There it was again.

Jude got out of bed and put on his robe. He had to know what was making the sound, otherwise he'd never be able to sleep. Tiptoeing along the hallway floor so as not to wake his mom, he grabbed a flashlight and shovel from the garage and snuck outside. The backyard might have been warm and cozy during the daylight hours, but at night insects chanted their secret songs and strange shapes lurked in the darkness. Jude dashed across the grass and shone his flashlight on Nibbles's grave.

His heart jumped like a startled cat.

The grave was open, revealing the cherry-red shoebox Jude had used as a coffin. Its lid had been torn to shreds. He bent down, angling the light, but saw no sign of the guinea pig's body.

Because she's not there anymore, Jude thought. *She clawed her way out.*

That was impossible, of course. Guinea pigs didn't come back to life. Unless . . . could he possibly have buried her alive? Her body had seemed stiff and cold when Jude found her, but it wasn't like he was a vet or anything.

What if he had made a mistake?

Jude imagined Nibbles waking in the darkness, her initial fear turning to rage as she vowed revenge against her former owner.

"Don't be an idiot," he said. "Nibbles is worm food. And even if she isn't, so what? It's just a dumb guinea pig. There's nothing to be scared—"

Something soft brushed against his bare ankle.

Jude screamed and fled inside the house. By the time he reached his bedroom, he had already begun to laugh at his own foolishness. There was no zombie guinea pig out to get him because he always forgot to feed her. It had just been a chipmunk or one of the mice that occasionally found its way into their attic.

Thinking of all the other animals that lived in his backyard, Jude developed a new theory that explained everything.

Something dug Nibbles up and ate her!

That had to be it. They saw opossums in their backyard all the time, even the occasional fox, and Jude had been too lazy to dig the hole very deep. A hungry predator must have smelled Nibbles's decaying body and dug her up—which explained the scratching noise he had heard earlier.

Serves her right for being such a boring pet, Jude thought with a grin.

Feeling better now, he turned over on his side and eventually fell asleep. He was awoken sometime later by a familiar sound.

Scritchscratch. Scritchscratch.

Jude opened his eyes. Something about the sound had changed. For a few moments he was too groggy to put his finger on the difference, and then the answer snapped into place.

The sound was coming from inside his room.

Totally alert now, Jude raised himself on one elbow and listened carefully. Something was scratching the wooden footboard at the end of his bed. He couldn't see anything unusual above the covers, so he slowly lifted them and looked down at his feet. Two glowing red eyes peered back. Nibbles's orange fur might have been matted with dirt, but there was no doubt it was her. She hissed, revealing all sorts of teeth that hadn't been there before, and bit his big toe. All of a sudden, Jude couldn't move. He couldn't scream. All he could do was watch as Nibbles took one tiny bite after another, starting at the bottom and working her way to the top.

For the first time ever, Jude did an excellent job of feeding his pet.

Alex tried to gauge Natacha's reaction as she read his story. She wasn't smiling, but that didn't mean anything. She hardly ever smiled. At the midway point, she crouched down and started to read faster. Alex couldn't tell if this was a good sign or a bad one. Maybe she couldn't wait to see what happened next. Or maybe she was skimming because she was bored.

It was only at the end, when he saw the look of disappointment on Natacha's face, that he knew for sure.

"I expected better," she said, shaking her head. "It's hard to believe you're the same boy who lulled Griselda to sleep with all those beautiful dark dreams."

Alex wilted beneath the criticism. As much as he hated to admit it, Natacha's opinion meant a lot to him.

"I didn't think it was that bad," he muttered.

"It wasn't that good, either."

"Well, I'm tired, okay! I mean, not really tired, I guess, because I'm actually sleeping right now, but—*none of this makes any sense!*" Alex turned away so Natacha couldn't see the tears forming in the corners of his eyes. "I just want to go home."

"Then you should have written a less predictable story. I could have told you the entire plot from start to finish after reading the first few paragraphs. I kept hoping you were going to throw some kind of twist in there, but nope. No surprises at all. I've read a thousand stories just like it."

Alex wasn't above taking constructive criticism, but this was a bitter pill to swallow.

"You've read a thousand scary stories about guinea pigs?" he asked, bristling.

Natacha scoffed. "Just yours—probably because every other horror writer was smart enough to realize that guinea pigs aren't scary. They're barely even pets. They're just . . . fuzzy slippers with delusions of grandeur. Besides, it wasn't the guinea pig part that made your story predictable. It was the plot. How many stories have you read where someone who was wronged in life comes back to take revenge?"

"One or two," Alex admitted. It was a lot more than that, but he wasn't about to give Natacha the satisfaction. "But those were *people* who came back for revenge, not guinea pigs. It's totally different."

"People or guinea pigs or Komodo dragons, the plot is still the same. Unless you can put your own spin on it, why tell it at all? Come on, Alex. You're better than this."

Alex wanted to argue, but he knew Natacha was right. There were parts of "Nibbles" that he liked, but it wasn't his most original effort. Unfortunately, it was about the best he could do these days.

"Maybe it's not a total loss," said Natacha, kneeling beside the grave. Simeon lay next to her, his massive paws hanging over the open edge. Witch and familiar stared intently into the hole. If Alex had been imprisoned almost anywhere else, this would have been the perfect opportunity to make a break for it. But where was he going to go? He couldn't escape his own mind. This thought threatened to push him into a pit of despair until he felt a reassuring nudge against his leg. Lenore. She had turned herself invisible to hide her presence.

Smart thinking, Alex thought, giving the cat a furtive pat. *Natacha has no idea she's here. We might be able to use that to our advantage.*

"Here we go," Natacha said, rubbing her hands together.

Dirt began to rise from the bottom of the grave like water from a well. In no time at all, the hole was completely refilled with dark soil. A thin stem poked its head out of the ground.

"Yes!" Natacha exclaimed. With surprising tenderness, she loosened the dirt to clear the stem's path. It was already six inches tall and growing fast. "Come into the world, little one!"

Moments later, yellow petals grew into place. Alex, who made it his business to know the names of things, was able to identify dozens of flowers. This one was easy: a dandelion.

"Did my *story* make that?" he asked in bewilderment.

Natacha nodded. "With the help of a few enchantments."

40

"Wow. How does that work? Why would you even—"

"Shh," Natacha said, raising a finger to her lips. "Let Simeon do his thing."

The jackal leaned forward and gave the flower a few delicate sniffs. He closed his eyes, like a wine connoisseur savoring a particularly complex bouquet, and gave a short, disappointed yip.

Natacha glared at Alex. "I figured it wouldn't be good enough," she said. "The dandelion gave it away. That's about as common as you can get."

"What are you *talking* about?" Alex asked, starting to get frustrated. He was tired of not understanding anything that was happening to him.

"Your boring story made a boring flower. That clear enough for you?"

"No! Nothing you're saying makes any sense at all!"

"Original, imaginative stories make good flowers. Those are the kind I need. Dull stories make"—she gave the dandelion a dismissive nod—"that. This will do for tonight, but I expect better next time."

Alex looked up at her with hopeful eyes. "Does that mean you're going to let me wake up now?"

"Hmm," Natacha said with a smirk. It had been a long time since Alex had cowered before her, and he suspected she wanted to savor the moment. "Maybe I should keep you here until you write a story I'm happy with. We do

41

have unlimited time at our disposal. What do you think, Simeon?"

The jackal yipped. Natacha sighed with disappointment and nodded.

"I suppose you're right," she said. "This kind of not-sleep can have unfortunate side effects, and we need that precious brain of yours in peak working order for a long time to come. But if your next story isn't more to my liking . . . well, don't think you're safe just because this is a dream. I have total control over when you wake up. Remember what it was like being stuck in this graveyard for just a few days? Now imagine that stretched out for years. The boredom! The loneliness! You'd wake up a stark, raving madman."

There were so many questions Alex wanted to ask. How was Natacha able to control his dreams? What did she want with his story flowers? But he didn't want to risk annoying the witch. If he did, she might not let him wake up—and right now, that was his first priority. Everything else could wait.

"Until tomorrow, then," Natacha said. "Just because you'll be able to do whatever you want during the daytime, don't start believing you're free. You're still my prisoner. And unlike my apartment, this isn't the type of prison you can escape. Everyone has to sleep sometime." She pinched his cheek. "I've missed you, storyteller. *Awake!*"

4

MORE THAN JUST A DREAM

After nearly changing her mind three times, Yasmin Khoury finally entered the Korean café. The air was redolent with the smells of coffee and freshly baked bread. Brightly lit display cases showcased baked goods such as red bean buns, strawberry cream soboros, and mocha bread. Yasmin slipped through a group of giggling teenagers drinking bubble tea and spotted Alex sitting at a small table. He was erasing something in one of his nightbooks.

It was the first time Yasmin had seen him in four months.

Alex had lost weight and gotten new glasses with a boxy black frame. His tousled hair stuck up in several places, and his beloved *Evil Dead* T-shirt, which featured a woman reaching for help while a monstrous hand dragged her beneath the ground, was beginning to fade from too many trips to the washing machine.

Seeing him after all this time made Yasmin smile. Maybe coming here had been a good decision after all.

"Hey," she said, taking a seat. "Whatcha writing?"

Yasmin leaned over the table and looked at the open notebook. A few lonely sentences peeked out through a muddy field of erasures.

"Nothing," Alex snapped, closing the nightbook. He nodded toward a plastic tray in the center of the table. "I got you a chocolate croissant. I know you prefer the kind with the almonds, but they were out. I told you we should have gone to the other place. It never gets this crowded."

"It's fine," Yasmin said. The other café was only a few blocks from Bayside Apartments, where she had once been imprisoned by a witch. As far as Yasmin was concerned, that was too close for comfort. "Love the new glasses."

"Stephen King had a pair like this," Alex said, blushing. "Not that I think I'm Stephen King. No one's Stephen King."

"I have the same glove as Francisco Lindor, and I'm definitely not as good as him."

"He hit a homer last night."

"You watched the game?" *Without me*, she almost added, and then realized how unfair that would be.

"A few innings," Alex said with a shrug.

An awkward silence fell between them. During the

summer, they had watched a ton of Mets games together while Yasmin patiently explained the rules. At first, she couldn't get Alex into it, and he had watched with the perplexed expression of someone trying to follow a foreign film without subtitles. It was only after Yasmin pointed out that a baseball season had actual story lines—teams who were bitter rivals, plot twists when a great player failed or a terrible player saved the day, a postseason climax—that Alex began to enjoy it.

"Cool nightbook," Yasmin said, just to say something. Alex had decorated the black-and-white composition book with pictures of a scary house at the top of a hill, a snarling werewolf, and a sleek black spaceship. "Did you ever show your stories to that teacher at your school? The one who runs the creative writing club?"

"Yeah. She said I have a lot of potential, but she'd prefer to see a personal narrative or realistic fiction. Horror's not her thing."

"Potential is good, right?"

"I guess. How are things with you?"

"Better," Yasmin said. "I rejoined the softball team. My grades are up, too."

"That's great. Are you still having trouble sleeping?"

For months after their escape from apartment 4E, Yasmin had been plagued by terrible nightmares. There had been doctor's visits, medication, time off from school.

45

Nothing helped. No matter what she tried, she just couldn't seem to leave the apartment behind. Finally, she realized why. Alex. Through no fault of his own, he was a living, breathing reminder of the experience she needed to forget.

If Yasmin truly wanted to move on, Alex couldn't remain a part of her life.

They had been walking home from the park when she told Alex their friendship had to end. He had listened quietly as she explained her reasons and said he understood. Part of Yasmin wished he had screamed and yelled and called her names. In any case, her plan had worked. Without the constant reminders that Alex unwillingly provided, she had been able to scrub the apartment from her mind until only a vague remnant remained, like a water stain on a table. After that, her life had gradually begun to return to normal, except for the Alex-shaped hole in her heart.

"Yasmin?" Alex asked.

She realized that she had been staring into space, lost in her thoughts.

"Sorry," she said. "No nightmares. I've been sleeping like a baby."

"I'm glad to hear it," Alex said, and she could tell he was genuinely happy for her. "I'm sorry Lenore's not here. I tried to get her to come, but—"

"She still hates me. I get it."

"She doesn't hate you. She misses you."

Yasmin had also parted ways with Lenore. It was hard to pretend the world was normal when you kept company with a magical cat.

"I know you wouldn't have texted me unless it was important," Yasmin said. "What's going on?"

Alex was easily the bravest person Yasmin knew, which made the fear in his eyes truly worrisome.

"Something happened," he said. "You're not going to like it."

An alarm went off in Yasmin's head. *Leave now,* she thought. *You don't want to be a part of this.* Except how could she just abandon Alex when it was clear he needed her help? He deserved better than that.

"Tell me," she said.

Alex removed his glasses and rubbed his eyes. He looked exhausted. "I had a dream. Or nightmare, I guess you'd call it. Which is weird for me. I used to have night terrors when I was little, but ever since I learned how to write, I don't dream at all. It's like I get all my fears out on the page so there isn't anything left when I fall asleep at night."

"But still. People have nightmares."

"Natacha was there."

Yasmin shrugged. "Oceans have sharks. Nightmares have Natachas."

"I'm not explaining this right," Alex said, running his

hands through his hair. "I don't mean I had a nightmare about Natacha. I mean I had a nightmare, and Natacha was there. The *real* Natacha."

Yasmin gave Alex a look of concern. His recovery from their horrific experience had been remarkably smooth. Now she wondered if the psychological trauma of those lost days was catching up to him at last.

"Natacha is dead," she said in a slow, calm voice. "You know that, right?"

"I'm not crazy."

"I didn't say you were. But dead is dead."

Alex scoffed. "Not in horror stories."

"This isn't a story. This is real life."

"You know what I've learned about 'real life' in the past year? Magic is real, witches exist, and 'Hansel and Gretel' is nonfiction. So, you'll have to excuse me if I've grown a teensy bit more flexible about what I'm willing to believe."

Yasmin understood the cold certainty in his eyes. For a long time, she had found it impossible to believe that the nightmare was truly over. She had to help him understand that Natacha was gone for good. Only then could he truly be free.

"Tell me about this dream," she said.

For the next twenty minutes, Alex told her a remarkable story about a dream graveyard where abandoned ideas grew into flowers. Yasmin didn't say a word. Occasionally she picked at the chocolate croissant. Mostly she just listened. It had been a long time since she had heard one of Alex's stories, and she was floored anew by his prodigious imagination.

"What do you think?" Alex asked when he was done.

Yasmin laughed. "I think my dreams are really boring compared to yours," she said. When Alex didn't smile, she added, "But I need to ask you a question. What makes more sense? A dead woman with no magical powers is reborn as a true witch, or a kid with a huge imagination has a nightmare?"

"You don't believe me," Alex said, stunned.

"I believe that you believe it. There was a time when I saw Natacha everywhere. In the hallways at school, in line at the grocery store, crouched at the end of my bed when I woke up in the middle of the night." Yasmin gave his hand a supportive squeeze. "What happened to us leaves scars, Alex—the kind you can't see. And it's not like we can talk to anyone about it. That makes it harder."

"We could talk to each other," Alex said with a thin smile. She noted the use of past tense: *could*, not *can*. A very Alex sort of dig. "She's back, Yasmin, whether you want to accept it or not. I could really use your help. We already beat Natacha once. We can do it again. But if you're not cool with that, I get it. I mostly just wanted to warn you. Because if she can come into my dream, she can come into yours."

"Take that back!" Yasmin screamed. Her voice cut through the conversations of the café, drawing curious stares. "Take that back right now!"

Alex gave her a sad, defeated look.

"Okay, Yas," he said. "I take it back. It's my stories Natacha wants. There's no reason for her to go after you."

Yasmin nodded and rose from her seat. "I have to go. Softball practice. I think we're going to make the playoffs this year! It was nice to see you again. I wouldn't worry too much about your nightmares. I'm sure they'll stop on their own. Mine did."

Alex looked like he was about to say something and sighed instead. "Good luck, Yasmin."

She exited the café. Main Street was packed with ordinary people going about their very ordinary business, and she basked in their shopping bags and cell phone conversations and crying children, feeling better by the minute. Behind the scenes, Yasmin's efficient mind had already begun building the necessary walls to protect her from harm. By the time she went to bed that night, she barely remembered her conversation with Alex at all.

5

THE THIRD NIGHT

Alex tried to stay awake as long as possible, but his previous visit to the story graveyard had drained his body in ways he didn't fully understand, and it was impossible to stave off sleep for long. Natacha was already there when he arrived, stretched out on a lawn chair. Her boots had been set to the side so she could paint her toenails. Simeon was lying next to her, chewing on something pinned beneath his paws. Alex caught a glimpse of a ravaged creature with golden scales and pink innards. It was still moving.

"I'm so glad you decided to come back," Natacha said, reaching forward to dot her pinkie toe. "Oh, that's right. You don't have a choice!"

Alex ignored her and started looking for a grave to unearth. Last night he had jumped at the first engraving he saw. He planned to put a little more thought into his next choice.

"What's with the mopey face?" Natacha asked. "This isn't so bad! One story a night. Do that, and your life continues, same as always. I won't bother you during the day. Grow up, get married, make little storyteller babies. I don't care. That's your time. But once you close your eyes at night, you're *mine.*"

Alex picked a tombstone engraved with a jack-o'-lantern and began to dig. Just like last time, the gravebook appeared right after he opened the lid of the coffin, and he tucked the book beneath his arm as he dropped into a suburban neighborhood on Halloween night. Candlelit jack-o'-lanterns stared at him from porch stoops, and dozens of trick-or-treaters roamed from house to house, filling their plastic pumpkins with candy. Alex found the setting charming but generic, making him think that this grave world hadn't come from a strong, specific idea, but a vague desire to write a Halloween story. In a way, that made things easier. Alex could basically write about anything he wanted, as long as it took place on October 31.

You can do this, he thought.

He found a seat on the front steps of an old Victorian and opened his gravebook, his metallic-tipped pen poised for action as soon as inspiration struck. More than likely, he would end up with more ideas than he could possibly use, and it would simply be a matter of choosing the best one. Halloween was his favorite holiday, after all.

Dream hours passed. Trick-or-treaters came and went.

His gravebook remained empty.

Alex tried changing positions—standing, lying down, jumping up and down—as though his body was a tree and the ideas simply needed to be shaken lose.

Nothing helped.

Finally, a little girl wearing a pirate costume skipped over to Alex and held out her plastic pumpkin.

"Trick or treat!" she exclaimed with a waxy smile. As with the cashier at Anything but Dogs!, her lips remained motionless.

"Sorry, kid," Alex said. "I don't have any candy."

"Trick or treat!" she repeated.

Alex lowered his voice to a conspiratorial whisper. "Say—you don't happen to know a good idea for a story, do you? Tell me, and I'll make you the main character. That's *way* better than candy. I'll even let you pick your name. Sound good?"

The pirate stared at him blankly with her unpatched eye. "Trick or treat!"

"That's all you can say, isn't it?" Alex asked.

She nodded and skipped off into the night.

After a few loops of the neighborhood, Alex finally came up with an interesting premise, but there was something about it that seemed familiar to him. In his experience, that meant one of two things. Either it was an old idea that he had never gotten around to writing (which was fine), or it was something he had seen or read (which was not). Alex lived in a world of ideas, and sometimes it was hard to remember which ones had originated with him. Normally he would have combed the internet to see if the story had already been created in one form or another, but since that wasn't an option, he decided to just write it and hope for the best. It was a laborious process, just like with "Nibbles," but at last he finished.

The gravebook burst into flames. Alex hoped that was a good sign.

Natacha was already reading the story when he returned to the graveyard. About midway through, she let out a long sigh and fixed him with a disbelieving glare.

"Are you *trying* to be unoriginal?" she asked.

"What are you talking about?" Alex asked defensively. "It's a good idea."

"It *was* a good idea when the first writer did it. Now it's a cliché. A useless, powerless cliché."

"You haven't even finished it yet."

"I don't need to. Let me tell you what happens. The kids put on their Halloween costumes, and they become their Halloween costumes. The boy in the werewolf mask becomes a werewolf. The girl wearing a cape and fangs

54

turns into a vampire." Natacha let out a long, exaggerated yawn. "Been there, done that."

"Yeah, but my version has a twist ending," Alex said, his cheeks burning. "See, once everything goes back to normal, we find out that Dennis is actually a . . ."

". . . monster in a person costume," Natacha said.

"I thought you didn't read it."

"I didn't need to. It was obvious what was going to happen from the first page."

Alex stood in stunned silence as they watched a new flower grow from the grave dirt: a white carnation. Simeon sniffed it and gave an apathetic yip, as though it wasn't even worth his time.

"A carnation," Natacha said, her lip curled with disgust. "You can buy a dozen of them in any supermarket. They might even be more common than dandelions." She lifted Alex's chin and looked him square in the eyes. "Are you screwing up these stories on purpose? Because let me make this clear. If you fail, I don't just let you go. That's not how this works."

"I'm doing the best I can," Alex insisted.

Natacha's expression softened the slightest bit. "I was afraid of that. Well, I don't know what's broken in that storyteller brain of yours, but you better fix it fast—or you're going to be stuck in this graveyard forever."

* * *

The next night, Alex picked an engraving of an alien planet, thinking a change of genre might help his chances, and dropped through the coffin into a bleak and desolate landscape. The atmosphere had a purplish tinge, and the clouds galloped away if he stared too long. He crossed a dune of black sand and saw a glass coffin hovering a few feet off the ground. It was surrounded by seven squid-like aliens making screeching noises that might have been weeping. They paid Alex little heed as he looked through the top of the glass and stifled a scream with his knuckle, not wanting to offend the mournful guardians. The creature sleeping inside the coffin might have been a beautiful princess by alien standards, but on Earth she was the stuff of nightmares.

I thought of this while I was watching a Disney movie with my little cousin, Alex remembered. Fairy tales were the chameleons of literature and could change their appearance to fit any genre, so Alex had thought it would be fun to retell one with a sci-fi twist. Clearly this planet was a riff on "Snow White," but that had never been his favorite, so he considered a few other options. "Beauty and the Beast" seemed like an easy fit—just switch out the main characters with a human and that thing in the glass coffin—but maybe that was *too* similar. How about "Rumpelstiltskin"? The miller's daughter could be a space pirate who traveled the galaxy searching for the imp's name in order to save her newborn child. Alex loved that idea, but it sounded like more of a novel than a short story.

He paced back and forth, running through every fairy tale he could think of, turning princes into robots and faithful steeds into teleportation machines. In the end, however, he couldn't settle on a single idea. Feeling frustrated, he decided to return to the graveyard and try his luck somewhere else. More out of curiosity than anything else, he picked a tombstone engraved with a single dot and began to dig.

This new coffin led to a shopping mall.

"Zombies," Alex told Lenore, who had finally joined him in the dream. "If there's a mall, there has to be zombies."

Alas, the mall was zombie free. The only thing Alex found that was remotely out of the ordinary was on the backlit mall directory. Instead of just one dot with YOU ARE HERE written beneath it, there were dozens of them.

According to the map, Alex was pretty much everywhere.

It was a creepy concept, but he couldn't figure out a way to develop it into a full-fledged story. Alex didn't want to return to the graveyard right away, however, so he found a seat at the abandoned food court and wrote a story about a lonely zombie who befriends a ghost. It was a vast improvement over his previous efforts, and Alex was bewildered when the gravebook didn't burst into flames—until he realized that he had forgotten to include the mall in his story.

He couldn't just write anything he wanted. It had to match the grave world in order to work.

After a brief return to the graveyard, Alex found himself in an old Victorian mansion and managed to piece together a story about a girl who moves to a haunted house. The flower that bloomed was an ordinary daisy that Simeon didn't even bother to sniff.

"Maybe I was wrong about you," Natacha said.

Those few words were far more worrying than her usual sarcastic quips. Natacha was beginning to lose faith. If Alex couldn't solve his storytelling woes soon, she'd just give up and leave him in this dream world forever.

Night three. Alex immediately grabbed his shovel and began hunting for the right grave world. He was determined to write a story that was original enough to satisfy Natacha. Part of this was simple self-preservation. He wasn't sure how many more chances Natacha was willing to give him. But there was also a degree of pride involved. *Maybe I was wrong about you*, Natacha had said. In other words: *I thought you were a great writer, but I guess I made a mistake.* The words bit deep. Alex had thought the very same thing about himself on countless occasions.

He wanted—no, needed—to prove Natacha wrong.

After deciding upon a cracked tombstone engraved with a stethoscope, Alex set to work, digging with furious abandon. *What's scary about going to the doctor?* he thought, trying to get a head start. Needles. That was an easy one, but overused. He needed to avoid clichés. Learning you had a horrible disease? Too realistic and sad. What about the stethoscope itself? What if it let you hear something else besides a heartbeat? Maybe there could be a—

Natacha appeared out of nowhere, breaking his train of thought. She was wearing sunglasses and a wide-brimmed black hat.

"Let me tell you what it's like to die," she said. "First things first. It hurts. Griselda ate me quick, but the mind does this thing at the end where it slows down and lingers, like it wants to savor those final moments, no matter how bad. I could feel every bone break, every muscle tear. I could even feel this small, inconsequential rock digging into my back. But the physical pain is nothing compared to the sheer anguish of knowing that the little light you cast for a few measly years is about to be turned off forever. Even the purest soul in the world—even you, Alex!— would kill their own mother for just another breath." She scoffed. "Not because life is so great, mind you. But it's a lot better than that terrifying mystery ready to pull you into the darkness forever."

Alex stared at her, mouth agape. "Thanks for sharing."

"I thought you'd like to know."

"Uh-huh," he replied. Since Natacha was in a talkative mood, he tried to gather some information. "So you were really dead, huh? How'd you manage to come back?"

Simeon took a step toward Alex and growled. Natacha rested her hand on the jackal and gave Alex a look over the top of her sunglasses. "That's on a need-to-know basis, storyteller," she said. "And you don't need to know." She pushed her sunglasses back into place and spun around in a circle. "Now let me tell you how it feels to *watch* someone die! The life slowly leaving their eyes is like the last bit of water draining from a tub . . . that's called a simile, by the way . . . and if you stare hard enough, you can—"

"Stop!" Alex exclaimed. "Why are you telling me this?"

"Because I'm trying to inspire you, storyteller! Guinea pigs? Trick-or-treaters? When did you get so *soft*? What happened to all that wonderful darkness you had back in my apartment?"

"Things are different now," Alex said.

"How?"

Alex ignored her and continued digging his hole. He wasn't about to tell Natacha that writing a story—any story—had become a struggle since the last time they met. She would ask why, and he didn't want to get into it.

"Ahh," Natacha said. "I should have realized it sooner.

Don't worry, storyteller. I know exactly what you need."

She whispered something to Simeon, who gave an eager yip and vanished. When the jackal returned a few minutes later, Yasmin was with him.

6

DOCTER

Yasmin found herself in a graveyard. She had no idea how she had gotten there. While her disoriented mind tried to slide the pieces together, she felt someone poking her arm.

"Yasmin," Alex said. "Is that really you?"

"Where are we?"

"My dream. The one I told you about."

"Dream? This isn't a dream." How could it be? The ground was solid beneath her feet. She even felt a little chilly in the thin red sweater she was wearing.

"I'm sorry," Alex said.

He pointed behind her at Natacha. The witch smiled and wiggled her fingers. Yasmin fell to her knees. She tried to scream, but all the air had been squeezed out of her lungs and the best she could manage was a sad whistling noise, like a dying balloon. The tombstones spun.

"Are you okay?" Alex asked, wrapping his arms around her. Yasmin shook him off. She was not okay. Natacha was alive again. Nothing could be okay anymore.

"It isn't fair!" Yasmin exclaimed. Her fear had—for this moment, at least—been eclipsed by a furious sense of injustice. "You're supposed to be dead! We escaped the apartment. We won!"

"You sure did," replied Natacha. "And I would have left you alone, except Alex here needs his little muse."

"I never said that!" Alex exclaimed.

"You didn't have to. I inferred. Now that the team's back together again, I'm expecting a truly spectacular story. If not, there will be serious consequences."

Yasmin ran, not sure where she was going, just trying to get as far from the witch as possible. A big black dog she hadn't noticed before nipped at her heels, tripping her up. She tumbled to the ground. Natacha laughed.

"Here," Alex said, helping Yasmin prop herself against a tombstone.

"When did Natacha get a dog?"

"It's a jackal. I didn't ask for Natacha to bring you here. I never wanted this to happen."

Alex looked like he was about to cry. Yasmin was still unsure what, exactly, was going on, but she was positive about one thing: Alex would have kept her far away from this if he could.

"I'm sorry I didn't believe you," Yasmin said.

"It's okay. If the situations were reversed, I probably wouldn't have believed you either."

"Yeah, you would have."

Alex held out his hand. Yasmin took it and got to her feet.

"Aww," Natacha said with a smug smile. "I've forgotten how adorable you two are when your lives are on the line."

Yasmin followed Alex to a partially exhumed grave. A stethoscope had been engraved into the tombstone. For a moment, she thought this meant the grave was the final resting place of a doctor, but then she remembered what Alex had told her in the café.

It wasn't a body that was buried here. It was an idea.

Alex continued to dig. A few moments later, a shovel appeared in Yasmin's hand, and she joined him. The coffin wasn't buried deep, and with the two of them working together, they were able to exhume it in a couple of minutes. Alex used his shovel blade to open the lid, and Yasmin found herself looking down a tree-lined dirt lane barely wide enough for a car.

A gray book materialized on the tombstone. Alex took it.

"How does this work?" Yasmin asked, looking through the coffin. "We just go down?"

"Sort of," Alex said. "That first step is a little tricky.

It looks like you're going down, but as soon as you pass through the portal you'll be standing on the ground. Does that make sense?"

"Not even a little bit." Yasmin glared at Natacha. "But it has to be better than staying here with her, so . . ."

She dropped through the opening. It was a strange sensation, just like Alex had said. Yasmin felt like she should be falling, but she somehow found herself standing on the road with the coffin right behind her. She saw Alex sit on the edge of the grave and dangle his feet, as though about to drop from a great height, and then he was standing right next to her, tottering from side to side. She held his arm while he steadied himself.

"I still haven't gotten used to that part," he said. "How did you make it look so easy?"

"I've always had good balance. Helps with baseball, field hockey, and crossing between dream worlds."

Alex laughed. "I won't lie. There's a part of me that's glad you're here. It's selfish, but it's true."

"Where's Lenore?"

"She kind of pops in and out. I get the impression this isn't the only dream she visits every night."

"That cat has a better social life than I do," said Yasmin. She looked up and down the road. It seemed impossible that it was only a dream—everything looked so *real*. "Where are we?"

"No clue."

"But this is your idea! How could you just forget it?"

"Do you remember every idea you've ever had?" Alex asked.

"Fair enough."

"Let's explore a little. That'll help me figure out what to write."

As in the graveyard, the painted moon cast more light than natural, allowing them to see clearly despite the darkness. They quickly realized that the road wasn't a road at all, but a long private driveway that led to a ramshackle yellow house set deep in the woods. The station wagon in the driveway made it clear that the house wasn't abandoned, though maybe it should have been. The front porch was sinking into the earth, and the broken roof looked like a giant had started the merciful process of stomping the house to dust and then decided he didn't want to get his feet dirty.

There was a piece of cardboard taped to the filthy front window. One word had been written on it in thick black Sharpie:

DOCTER

"I remember where this idea is from!" Alex exclaimed. "We were driving to one of my brother's football tournaments, and we passed this old house with a sign in the window. DENTIST. It got my mind going. I mean, what kind of dentist would work in a house like that?"

"Not the kind I want to go to."

"Exactly. I changed it to *docter* because . . . I don't know. When I get an idea from something in the real world, I feel like I have to tweak it to make it mine. And I spelled it wrong because I thought it would make it creepier."

"Like with *Pet Sematary*."

Alex's eyes lit up. He had recommended the book to Yasmin right before they stopped talking. "Did you read it?"

Yasmin looked down at her feet. "Watched the movie."

"Which version—1989 or 2019? Because there are pros and cons to each—"

"Game face, Mosher," she said, shaking him by the shoulders. "What happens in this creepy doctor story of yours?"

"Um . . . well . . ."

"You do *know*, don't you?"

"Creepy house with a doctor sign! That's as far as I got! I couldn't think of anything else, so I forgot about it."

Yasmin was surprised. The Alex she knew wouldn't have given up so easily. When he was stuck on an idea, he was like a dog with a pull toy, tugging at it until it came free. She remembered all the erasure marks she had seen in his nightbook. *What's up with him?* she wondered.

"No worries," Yasmin said, forcing herself to remain calm. Alex already looked stressed enough, and she didn't want to make it any worse. "Let's check this place out. I bet there's something inside just waiting to inspire you."

Unfortunately, the house was drab and ordinary. Only one of the rooms looked like it belonged in a doctor's office. Here they found an examination table, charts that showed various parts of the body, and a glass jar full of odd-shaped lollipops. Yasmin checked a few drawers and cupboards. They were mostly empty, though she did find a coffee can filled with rusty pennies.

"This mean anything to you?" she asked, shaking the can.

Alex shrugged and hopped up on the examination table. A cloud of dust rose into the air. "What kind of doctor is this?"

"A weird one."

Alex nodded. "That's probably why he has to work out of his house. The type of medicine he practices isn't accepted by the medical community."

"Why does the doctor have to be a *he*?" Yasmin asked with raised eyebrows.

"He doesn't. Maybe it's a she. Or an it. I was just thinking *he* because I was in a Dr. Frankenstein frame of mind."

"So he or she or it brings dead people back to life?"

"Nah. There are too many stories like that already. Not just *Frankenstein*. H. P. Lovecraft wrote a story about a doctor named Herbert West who—"

"You're not being graded on originality, Alex."

"Actually, I am. My stories haven't been creative enough to grow the kind of flower Natacha wants. That's why she brought you here. She thought you could help—which does make sense. I mean, the last time I wrote anything good was back in the apartment."

Uh-oh, Yasmin thought, putting this comment together with her earlier concerns. She had been on enough sports teams to know when someone's confidence had taken a serious enough blow that it was affecting their performance. Until this point, it hadn't occurred to her that it could work the same way with writing, but why not? She had always believed that talent was a little overrated. Most of doing anything was just believing you could do it.

"You're being too hard on yourself," Yasmin said. "You've written plenty of good stories since we escaped. What was the name of that one I liked? With the tire swing?"

"'Tire Swing.'"

"That's the one! So good. And there was another one." She snapped her fingers, trying to think of the title. "The house that keeps growing a little more each day . . ."

"'Square Footage,'" Alex said. He managed a smile.

69

"That one's not too bad."

"Not too bad? It was great! I read it to my parents, and they thought it was from a real book."

"Really?"

Yasmin nodded. It had been her six-year-old cousin, but close enough. The important thing was that Alex looked slightly less distraught. What she had done was little more than a Band-Aid, but hopefully it would be enough for now.

They tossed a few more ideas back and forth, and then Alex decided it was time to get started. Yasmin didn't have anything to do at that point, so she wandered out to the front yard and sat on the hood of the station wagon. There wasn't a star in the sky. She looked back toward the sign in the window: DOCTER. It wasn't something you would see from the road, and even if you did see it, you wouldn't stop. No one would come here unless they already knew about the doctor and were desperate for help.

"Huh," Yasmin said.

She reentered the house. Alex was sitting at the kitchen table, exactly where she had left him. He hadn't written a word. Either he was having trouble coming up with an idea, or her pep talk hadn't worked as well as she'd hoped.

"I asked you once how you decided who should be the main character of a story," Yasmin said, "and you told me it's whoever gets themselves into the most trouble."

"An active character," Alex said. "Yeah. That's kind of what I'm having trouble with right now. This doctor, the way I'm imagining him, he just stays here all day treating patients."

"Exactly," Yasmin said. "He's not getting in trouble. He's causing it. So I actually don't think the story is about the doctor."

Alex's eyes lit up. "It's about a patient!"

As Yasmin left the house, she heard Alex's pen scratch out the first words.

7

YASMIN TAKES A WALK

It was eerily quiet outside. Yasmin had always thought of dreams as a world where anything could happen, but this place seemed firmly rooted in reality. She watched a blue jay settle on a branch and fly off again. Was the bird part of Alex's original idea? If not, how had it gotten here?

The questions seemed too big for Yasmin to ask, let alone answer.

Time passed. Occasionally she checked to see how Alex was doing and saw him hunched over the gravebook, deep in his dream within a dream within a dream. She tried not to bother him. The quicker he finished, the better.

Except we'll be back here tomorrow night, won't we? Yasmin thought with a sinking heart.

She couldn't focus on that. If she did, it would be like setting down a welcome mat for her fears. She needed a distraction. A task. Alex had his puzzle to solve—what could she contribute? If they were going to be spending more time in these grave worlds, it was probably a good idea to learn as much about them as possible.

She decided to explore.

The driveway was boring, and there was nothing of interest inside the house. That left the woods. Most sections were too thick to enter, but she found a narrow path behind the house. The painted moon imbued the trail with a gentle glow, giving it a magical, storybook quality. It was practically begging her to explore it—which only heightened Yasmin's caution. She remembered how Natacha had tempted her into apartment 4E with the smell of her sito's cooking and wondered if the woods were playing a similar game.

"It'll be fine," Yasmin said as she took her first steps along the trail. "This isn't a witch's apartment. It's Alex's mind. He would never hurt me."

Fortunately, the trail was easy to follow, with none of the branching paths that made it so easy to get lost in a real forest. She wondered if she would reach a border at some point—an impasse of trees or maybe just a white void. After all, the seed of this world had been a mere sign in a window. How big could it have grown?

The path, however, showed no sign of ending.

She walked for some time, doing periodic checks to

make sure she could still see the house. At a certain point, it stopped getting any farther away. *That can't be right,* Yasmin thought. She did a light jog for thirty seconds, and sure enough, no matter how far down the path she traveled, the house refused to recede any farther in the distance. It was a sneaky border, but a border nonetheless.

Yasmin returned to the house.

"Where'd you go?" Alex asked, lowering his pen.

"I took a walk. I was curious how big the world was. There's a section out there where you could walk forever and never move forward."

"I came across a few areas like that in the graveyard. Like a treadmill, right?"

"Yeah." She peeked over his shoulder. "How close are you to being done? This place gives me the creeps."

"Almost there. I got stuck trying to think of a synonym for poisoned."

"Why do you need a synonym for poisoned? Poisoned is a perfectly good word. Here, let me prove it to you. 'Yasmin poisoned Alex because he didn't finish his story quick enough.'"

"'Toxic'?" Alex pondered, checking his work. "No. That doesn't sound right so close to 'noxious.' Unless I change 'noxious' to a different word . . ."

"Alex!"

"Fine! Poisoned it is." He settled back in his chair and

crossed his arms behind his head. "Now all I have to do is figure out the perfect ending."

"Perfection is overrated. Just write, 'And then I woke up. It was all a dream.' I always do that in school. Works every time."

Alex looked like she had asked him to eat a marshmallow-and-slug sandwich. Yasmin rolled her eyes and sat in the living room, giving him space to work. A few moments later, she heard the scratching of Alex's pen. It started slowly and rose to a near frantic level, which seemed promising. Suddenly, there was silence. Yasmin poked her head into the kitchen, intending to give Alex another nudge along the path of imperfection, but she could see from the way he was smiling that no further encouragement was needed.

"Done," he said, pushing his chair back just as the gravebook burst into blue flames.

"Your story!" Yasmin screamed.

She started toward the kitchen sink, intending to fill a glass with water, but Alex stopped her.

"Don't worry," he said. "That's just the gravebook transferring its contents to the tombstone. Totally normal."

"Totally," Yasmin said, staring at the pile of ashes. The house began to rumble. "Is that normal, too?"

"Yup. The grave world is destroying itself since I don't need it anymore." A crack split the wall and kept growing. "Although now that I think about it, I'm usually a lot closer to the coffin when I finish my story, so . . ."

They ran outside. The screaming wind was felling trees like a rampaging troll. Yasmin and Alex sprinted toward the graveyard. The ground felt strangely unstable, like ice that might not be thick enough to cross. Yasmin ran in a state of terror, imagining that her next footfall might crack the ground and send her spiraling into some kind of bottomless dream pit. Fortunately, the ground held, and they finally reached the coffin, which stood as still as a mailbox on a calm summer day. For one reason or another, the wind couldn't touch it.

Alex leaped through the opening, but Yasmin paused a moment to take a quick look behind her. A giant tear had appeared in the sky and was sucking up the world like a black hole. The doctor's house was gone. Most of the trees had vanished as well, and the few that remained were already skyborne, leaving behind nothing but barren dirt. Yasmin stepped through the opening and nearly fell straight back again—she had forgotten that she needed to climb to reach the graveyard. Fortunately, Alex grabbed her in time, and the two tumbled across the grass to safety. After taking a moment to gather her senses, Yasmin got to her feet. Natacha was standing over the grave, entranced by the dying world. Her back was facing them.

Push her! Yasmin thought.

She could picture it clearly. Two steps, maybe three.

Pause just long enough to set her feet. Line up her hands with Natacha's shoulder blades. Shove. Close the coffin. It would be over in seconds. Sure, they'd be the most terrifying seconds of Yasmin's life, but that was a small price to pay. She could end this, once and for all.

All . . . she had to do . . . was move.

Impossible.

It would have been easier for Yasmin to roll a boulder up a hill. Fear and doubt locked every joint in place. What if Natacha turned at the last moment? What if Yasmin didn't push hard enough? What if this oh-so-convenient opportunity was nothing but a trick? When Yasmin managed to move at last—a pathetic, wobbly half step in the general direction of the grave—Simeon leaped in front of her, blocking her path. There was the slightest smirk on his face, as though he knew what she had been thinking.

Natacha slammed the coffin lid into place and turned to face the tombstone. It had grown taller to allow the story now engraved into its surface.

Staying as far from the witch as possible, Yasmin crept forward and started to read.

CAST

I stumbled into the house, cradling my swollen arm like a dead pet. My dad took one look and knew the usual bag of ice wasn't going to cut it this time, so he fashioned a sling from one of Mother's old scarves and took me to the clinic. The woman at the desk turned down his insurance because it had expired, my dad being out of work for some time now, so we drove to this yellow house at the end of a long country road. Taped to one of the windows was a piece of cardboard with DOCTER written in thick black marker.

I asked my father if he was sure about this. He told me to get out of the truck.

The man who answered the door wore a starched white shirt and a string tie. The skin of his face looked hard, like a mannequin brought to life. I thought if I rapped his cheek with my knuckles it would make a knock-knock sound. He ushered me into a room and told Father to wait outside. My father did not argue.

As soon as the door was closed, the doctor placed his ear to my wrist, as though listening for a heartbeat, and proclaimed it was broken in two places. He searched through dusty cupboards until he found the mason jar he was looking for and unscrewed its rusty lid. A powerful stench filled the room. The doctor dumped the contents of the jar into a clay bowl. It was a chunky concoction that looked like spoiled milk and smelled even worse. My binding poultice, the doctor called it, and asked how I had hurt myself. I started to tell him the same lie about falling off my bike that I had told my dad, but the doctor's unflinching eyes squeezed the truth from me.

"I was at the big playground. There's this tunnel slide there that runs down from the top of a really high tower. These three boys forced me onto the outside of it and told me to climb down. I might have made it, but they started throwing rocks at me and I fell off."

The doctor nodded with a bored expression, as though my story was just a different version of a tale he had heard many times before. He took a brush with a red-stained handle and spread the poultice over my skin. The smell made my eyes water, but it sucked away the pain.

"I wish those boys would die," I said.

The doctor smiled his plastic smile and gave me a home-made lollipop with an unfamiliar taste. My father reentered and offered the doctor a few limp dollar bills from his wallet.

"Payment comes later," the doctor said.

By the time I got home, the poultice had hardened into a cast.

* * *

I told the kids at school the same made-up story I told my father. I was too scared to tell the truth and risk the wrath of those three boys. Peter. Kyle. Raymond. Plus I hoped that by not tattling I'd earn myself a reprieve from their daily torments. In the long run, the broken arm might be worth it.

Just before lunch, Peter stopped me in the hall and told me he was sorry, making me think my plan was working. The thing about me and Peter is we used to be friends back when Mother was still alive. And he hadn't thrown rocks like the others. He had just watched and done nothing. I told him it was okay and let him sign my cast. I had been asking people all morning, but there was still plenty of room.

It soon became clear that Raymond and Kyle did not harbor similar regrets. As we were lining up for recess, Raymond shoved me over Kyle's outstretched leg. I landed on my bad wrist, and though I'm ashamed to say it, I cried.

I looked up and saw Peter laughing harder than anyone.

The moment I got home I took a black Sharpie and crossed Peter's name off my cast. That night my wrist began to itch something awful. I tried to slide a pencil beneath the cast to scratch it but couldn't get inside. It was like the cast had attached itself to my arm.

It was a long time before I finally fell asleep. I had strange dreams.

* * *

Peter wasn't in school the next day. In math I found out why. He had fallen off his skateboard and smashed his face up good. Rumor was they had to stitch him up so bad he looked like Frankenstein's monster.

I could say I felt bad, but I'd be lying.

Unfortunately, Peter's absence did not improve my situation with the other two. At recess, Kyle and Raymond pinned me down while Kyle wrote LOSER on my cast. Then, laughing so hard snot exploded out his nose, he added his name in capital letters.

I didn't wait until I got home. I crossed out KYLE while watching some boring video about butterflies in science. When the screaming started, Mr. Simmons ran out the door and we all followed. Kyle had fallen down the stairs. His leg was bent in a way no leg was supposed to bend.

My arm itched.

I convinced myself that it was a coincidence, that there surely couldn't be any connection between the crossed-out names and the accidents that had befallen my tormentors. Still. Wouldn't it be interesting to see what might happen? I found Raymond the next day and felt a thrill as he avoided my gaze. There was fear in his eyes. Fear. Of me!

I held out a black Sharpie.

Raymond looked at Kyle's name and Peter's name and the way they had been crossed out and made no move to take the marker.

"You don't have to if you're scared," I said.

That did the trick. Raymond yanked my arm toward him and signed his name. I waited until I got home and used scissors instead of a marker, slashing away until no remnant of those poisoned letters remained. I cut so deep that I opened a slit in the cast, releasing a noxious smell that burned my nostrils.

I tried not to think about it.

The next day was a Saturday. My father read about what happened to Raymond in the paper and sat me down at the table to give me the sad news. Somehow, I managed not to smile.

By the next week, the itching had gotten so bad that we returned to the yellow house. The doctor—if that's what he really was—placed his ear to the cast and nodded with approval.

"Let's see what we've made here," he said.

He tapped the cast three times, and it broke apart like a shell. My new arm was black and shiny with three barbed spikes. As my father screamed, I turned it before me and saw the mouth that had grown in my forearm. Something was clenched between its terrible teeth. The doctor plucked this object away and regarded it with satisfaction: a strange red coin inscribed with letters I had never seen before and hoped to never see again.

My new mouth took a gasp of air. I could feel its hunger and knew I would have to feed it soon.

"Paid in full," the doctor said.

He dropped the coin into an old coffee can filled with them.

Yasmin finished the story. Natacha was still reading, her face mere inches from the tombstone. *Too vain for glasses*, Yasmin thought with a snicker. But wait. Was far-sightedness something that carried over into dreams? And where was the real-world Natacha right now? Asleep in her bed, or staring into space, lost in a magical trance?

Yasmin felt a tug at her sleeve.

"What did you think?" Alex whispered, unable to meet her eyes. "As I was reading it, I saw a whole bunch of things I wanted to change. Only it's written in stone. Like, literally."

"It was really good," Yasmin said, giving his arm a reassuring squeeze.

Alex brightened. "The story was meant to be about the patient, not the doctor—just like you said. It seems so obvious now, but I never would have figured it out if it wasn't for you."

Yasmin shrugged as though it were nothing, but inside she felt a burst of pride. Although she had no desire to write her own stories, she loved brainstorming with Alex. It was like helping to design a house and letting someone else do the work of building it.

"Not bad, storyteller," Natacha said. "Until you get to the ending, that is. In a way, that makes this even worse than your other efforts. At least those were disappointing from the start. With this one, you actually got my hopes up."

"What's wrong with the ending?" Alex asked.

"It doesn't make any sense. The boy's arm grows a mouth that gives the doctor some weird coin? What's that all about?"

"The doctor isn't human," Alex said. "He's a demon who's been imprisoned on earth until he pays off his debt. Every time he gets a patient to do something bad, he gets a coin as a reward. When the coffee can is all filled up, he can return home to his demon dimension. It makes *perfect* sense."

"Too bad none of that information was actually in the story," Natacha said.

"The ending wouldn't be creepy anymore if I explained it to death. Weird fiction is about *not* understanding."

Natacha turned to Yasmin. "Sounds like he's just making excuses, doesn't it?"

"I thought the ending was perfect," Yasmin said. Truth be told, she had also been confused, but she didn't want to derail her friend's fragile self-confidence by admitting it.

"Well, our opinion doesn't matter," the witch said, kneeling next to the grave with Simeon by her side. The hole had refilled itself, and a tall flower encased in a white shell had grown into place. Natacha tapped it with a fingernail. The shell broke apart, exposing a drooping iris with segmented red petals.

Simeon did his sniff test and gave an energetic yip. Natacha sighed with relief.

"We've never seen a flower like this one before," she said. "It wasn't a perfect story, but it *was* imaginative. A definite step in the right direction."

"Now who's the one being confusing?" Alex asked. "What are the flowers for? Why are we here?"

Natacha smiled wickedly.

"Awake," she said.

8

QUESTIONS WITHOUT ANSWERS

Alex woke up with his pajamas drenched in sweat. After a long shower, he texted Yasmin and suggested they talk in person. They were both craving warmth and sunlight, so they decided to meet at a park instead of a café.

"Rise and shine," he told Lenore, who was napping as usual. Since escaping the apartment, she had grown accustomed to a lifestyle that involved doing as little as possible, even by cat standards. Alex's dad—who believed she was a stray his son had rescued in downtown Flushing—called Lenore "the laziest animal he had ever seen." While Alex knew there was some truth to this, he preferred to think of her as enjoying a well-deserved retirement after a life of magical servitude.

Right now, however, Lenore was refusing to open her eyes. Alex gently tugged her long, distinctive tail. Lenore made a low noise in her throat and whacked him with it.

"Suit yourself," Alex said, already walking away. "I was going to the park and thought you might want to come."

That got Lenore's attention. The park was one of her favorite places. She loved stretching out on the grass and watching dogs get hit in the face with flying discs or fuzzy green balls. Sometimes Alex swore he could hear her laughing.

She followed him out of the room.

"Knew you couldn't resist," he said. "One other thing. Yasmin's going to be there." Lenore started back toward the bedroom, but Alex blocked her path. "I know you were in my dream last night and refused to show yourself because she was there. You need to get over it. If we're going to survive, we have to work together—just like last time."

Lenore swept through his legs, showing Alex exactly what she thought of *that* idea, and sauntered down the stairs. Alex followed her. He had spent his entire childhood living in an apartment and still had trouble believing his family had an actual house now. It wasn't much to look at, but he loved every wobbly step and sagging floorboard. His dad had even set up a few simple shelves so he could have his own miniature library in the basement. It was practically heaven.

He went out to the backyard—a backyard!—where his mom was pulling the weeds that always grew between the cracks of their tiny concrete patio.

"I'm going to the park," Alex said. "See you later!"

Mrs. Mosher wiped the sweat from her brow and gave him a worried look. "With who? Eddie?"

"Yasmin."

His mom yanked out a weed. "You friends with that girl again? After she dropped you like a bag of bricks?"

"I'm not sure. It's complicated."

"It's actually the simplest thing in the world. You're either friends or you're not friends. But I guess that's something you have to learn for yourself." She started to remove her gloves. "Why don't I drive you? I don't like you walking there alone."

"I'm not alone, Mom. Lenore's coming with me!"

Lenore puffed out her chest.

"Yeah, she's a regular guard cat," Mrs. Mosher said, rolling her eyes. "Let me get my keys."

Alex kissed her on the cheek.

"I'm *fine*, Mom. I'll be home at five."

"Four. On the dot. And text me when you get there and when you leave."

"Promise." Alex lifted the latch of the back gate but paused before leaving. "Did you and Dad read that story I gave you yet?"

A guilty look crossed Mrs. Mosher's face. "Not yet. We've been so busy with the new house. But soon, promise."

"Sure," Alex said. He might have commented that they hadn't missed any of his brother's football games since moving, but he decided to let it go. It was nothing new, and there was no sense making his mom feel bad.

The park was packed. Little kids chased each other across the grass, teenagers talked trash on the basketball court, and an elderly man did tai chi in his bare feet. Alex found Yasmin on the aluminum stands overlooking the baseball field, watching a Little League team run drills. She brightened the moment she saw Lenore and held out her arms.

"Get over here, you. It's been forever!"

Lenore spun around with a dramatic swoop of her tail and went hunting for comedic canines.

"That cat sure can hold a grudge," Yasmin said.

"You hurt her feelings," replied Alex, taking the seat next to her. "I guess after everything you've been through together, she figured you were friends for life."

Yasmin gave him a long look.

"So how are we getting out of this one?" she asked.

"The dream thing? Easy. We'll just never sleep again."

"Live on coffee and Mountain Dew?"

"Exactly."

"Sweet. Problem solved. Want to get ice cream?"

Alex checked for Lenore and found the cat resting beneath the shade of an oak tree. A little boy wearing a blue cap was pointing and laughing at her. "Fat cat!" he shouted. "That rhymes! Cat, fat. Fat cat!"

Lenore turned invisible. The boy screamed and ran away.

"At least with the apartment, we knew what we needed to do," Yasmin said. "Get out. It was just a question of how. But this? I don't even know where to begin."

"When I'm having trouble finishing a story, I retrace my steps and read the entire thing from the beginning. Sometimes I can't tell what's wrong, exactly, but I can sense where things feel *off*. That's usually a good place to start."

"This whole situation feels off. How is Natacha even *alive*?"

They threw around a few theories, trying to make sense of her improbable resurrection. As they talked, Alex glanced over at Lenore, who was visible again. The boy in the blue cap had returned to the oak tree with his mother and was jabbing an accusing finger at the cat. Lenore rubbed her head against the mother's leg and acted like a complete sweetheart. As soon as the mother turned her back, however, Lenore vanished. The boy screamed, but by the time the mother had spun around, Lenore was visible again. The cat watched with a mischievous grin as the mother yelled at her son for making up stories.

"I don't think I can bring Lenore to the park anymore,"

Alex said, massaging his brow. "So, it's not even that Natacha is alive. She seems to have legit powers now. How did *that* happen?"

"No clue," Yasmin said. She removed two bottles of water from her bag and tossed one to Alex. "Listen, we might not ever figure out how Natacha came back to life, or where her magic is coming from, so let's focus on what we know. Natacha is alive. She wants you to turn your old ideas into stories. When you do, flowers grow."

"Yeah, but not all flowers are created equal. Natacha liked the one last night because it was unique. My first few stories created boring, ordinary flowers."

"Was 'Cast' better?"

"It was definitely more imaginative, at least. I think that's the key ingredient. It's like fertilizer or something. The more original the story, the more original the flower."

"Still doesn't explain why she needs them, though," Yasmin said.

"It might be how she's getting her powers. Natacha's an expert at turning magical plants into enchanted oils."

"Except if these story flowers are her new source of magic, how did she get into your dreams in the first place?"

"Good point."

"What else do we know?"

Alex thought for a moment. "Natacha has a new familiar."

"The dog."

"Jackal. Maybe we can convince him to help us, like Lenore."

Yasmin shook her head. "He seems fiercely loyal to his master."

"So did Lenore, at first."

"Simeon's different. Lenore was always testy, but even before we teamed up, I never got the impression she wanted to hurt me. I don't feel the same way with Simeon. There's no warmth in his eyes at all."

Alex took a sip of water. The sun was beating down on the back of his neck, and his body ached all over. Spending so much time in the story graveyard was taking a toll. It was like he hadn't slept at all.

"We've only seen Natacha in dreams," he said. "But where's the flesh-and-blood version? She must be holed up somewhere."

"You think she's living in the apartment again?"

Alex shook his head. "Someone new lives there. My parents told me."

"For real?"

"It's just a normal apartment now. But we should probably check it out, just in case."

Yasmin's eyes grew large. "Good luck with that. I am never stepping foot in that building again."

Alex didn't try to change her mind. Yasmin refused to

even talk about the apartment. He'd never convince her to return in person.

"I wish there was someone we could ask for help," he said. "That's how it works in horror movies. The heroes hit a roadblock, so they consult an expert in the supernatural. An exorcist, or a professor, or a vampire hunter—whatever. But people like that don't exist in the real world. We're on our own."

"We might be able to trick Natacha into telling us something she shouldn't," Yasmin suggested. "It worked last time."

"I tried that, but she seems more cautious now. I guess she doesn't want to make the same mistake twice."

"Speaking of mistakes," Yasmin said, "when Natacha was looking down into the grave world, I thought about pushing her. I should have. I just couldn't work up the courage."

Alex shook his head. "You made the right decision. If we're going to get out of this, we need to be smart, not impulsive. Our safest bet is to give Natacha exactly what she wants until we figure out a plan. I just wish I was in a better writing place. I've been having such a hard time since we escaped the apartment."

"Why is that? You're such an awesome writer. Nothing's changed."

"The apartment changed everything. I'll never be that good again."

"What do you mean?"

Alex felt a surprising jolt of anger. It had taken months before he finally figured out why he had lost confidence in his writing, and his first instinct had been to tell Yasmin— except by then she had bowed out of his life. Now he didn't want to tell her at all. Maybe it was vindictive, but she'd have to earn his trust again first.

"I have to run," he said, breaking an awkward silence between them. "I promised my mom I'd be home by four. She freaks out if I'm even a minute late."

Yasmin got to her feet. "I have to go, too," she said, not meeting his eyes. Alex could tell he had hurt her feelings by refusing to confide in her. She paused at the bottom of the bleachers and glanced back over her shoulder. "Tell Lenore I said goodbye. I hope she can forgive me one of these days."

She cut across the baseball field and left the park. When the coast was clear, Lenore came over to sit by Alex's side. The cat gave him a pitying, protective look: *Don't be fooled into thinking she's your friend again.* It reminded Alex of his mother's reaction when he said he was hanging out with Yasmin. They were worried he would get hurt. Alex saw their point. Sure, Yasmin was acting like his friend right now, but what choice did she have? She needed him. The moment this was over, she'd probably never talk to Alex again.

Work together, he cautioned himself, *but don't get too close. She's not a forever type of friend.*

Alex started home. The park was emptier than when he had arrived, the sun lower in the sky. In just a few hours, he'd be in the graveyard again, struggling to come up with a story. He hoped he was up to the task.

9

KENNY'S BIRTHDAY PARTY

After dropping into a new grave world, Alex and Yasmin opened the side gate of a house and entered the backyard. Tethered balloons jerked in the breeze, and a banner strung between two oak trees proclaimed, HAPPY 8TH BIRTHDAY, KENNY! The theme of the party, judging from the brightly colored favors strewn across several long tables, was a movie called *Frisbee Man*. A sheet cake was topped with a square-jawed figure wielding a flying disc.

"Frisbee Man?" Yasmin asked.

Alex grinned. "I remember him! When I was little, I made up all these comic books called 'The Adventures of Frisbee Man!' I used to staple them together and leave them around the house for my parents to find. I don't remember too much, just that his Flying Disc of Doom used to glow whenever evil was near."

"Well, apparently he had a sidekick," Yasmin said, lifting a paper cup with a picture of Frisbee Man's stalwart companion, a robotic golden retriever named Fetch. Alex felt Lenore's tail whack him in the leg. She still refused to show herself in front of Yasmin, so this was the only way to make her displeasure felt.

"Okay, it's pretty obvious why this tombstone was engraved with a birthday cake," Yasmin said, "but this place doesn't seem so scary. It's actually kind of nice."

"I know," Alex said, confused. "Let's chill here for a while and see if we can figure it out."

A group of kids, most of them wearing cone-shaped birthday hats, stormed out of the house. Their movements were stiff and jerky.

"Eww," Yasmin said as the kids found seats on the grass. "Are those walking mannequins or something?"

"Wax figures. Since they're just side characters, I never thought about them too carefully—that's why they look so bad. Check out the kid with the birthday crown, though. That must be Kenny. He looks more realistic."

"Because you gave him a name. This mind of yours has its own kind of logic, doesn't it?"

"Like a story," Alex said.

Shortly afterward, an old man with a drooping mustache entered the backyard, wheeling a case that identified him as FRED THE MAGIC GUY. While the kids sat in creepy silence, occasionally fidgeting just for show, the magician set up a small table and began to perform his routine. It was painful to watch. Fred couldn't get his handkerchief to change color, accidentally revealed the hidden panel of a magic box, and pulled a carrot out of his hat instead of a rabbit.

"I feel bad for this poor guy," Yasmin said.

"Same here," replied Alex, already forming a story in his head. Maybe the old man had once been a great magician and was simply past his prime. In his younger years, he hadn't been Fred the Magic Guy. He had been Federico the Stupendous! His performances had filled entire opera houses. He had entertained presidents, kings, emperors. But something had happened, and the magic that had served Federico so well throughout his entire life had suddenly gone dry. Now here he was, at the end of his illustrious career, doing tricks for a bunch of spoiled brats.

Is that my story? Alex wondered.

He didn't think so. The plot felt too big for just a few pages. It would be like trying to cram an entire wardrobe into a single suitcase.

"Any ideas yet?" Yasmin asked.

"Nothing I can use. Let's keep watching."

Fred finished his show and departed to scattered applause. A young woman with long, frizzy hair took his place, smiling and waving to the kids like a kindergarten teacher after three cups of coffee. She started to unpack a guitar from a purple case covered with flower stickers.

"Who's this lady?" Yasmin asked.

"Some kind of singer, I guess," Alex said. He gasped as realization set in. "I know what this grave world is about! I always found the people who perform at birthday parties a little scary. Magicians, puppeteers, face painters—that whole crew. I wanted to write a story about one of them. I just never figured out which one."

Yasmin laughed. "So this is an audition to see who's creepy enough to be in your story."

"Basically."

"That's wild," she said, settling into her seat. Suddenly, her smile vanished. "Wait. Are there going to be clowns? I'm out of here if there are going to be clowns."

"Nah. Clowns have already been done to death by authors way better than me."

"You sure?"

"Totally."

The singer sat on a tall stool. She announced that her name was Ms. Sunshine and that she loved them all. After playing a few opening chords on her guitar, she sang the "Please and Thank You" song. This was immediately followed by an annoyingly catchy tune called "Pants on Fire," about the importance of telling the truth.

"I miss the terrible magician," Yasmin muttered.

"Me too."

"You notice how all her songs teach a lesson? What if in your story the kids were forced to follow her rules no matter what? So like after hearing this song, they were incapable of lying to their parents anymore."

"That's not bad. Do the parents know about Ms. Sunshine's powers?"

"You tell me. Is it a better story if they do or don't?"

Alex grinned. "How about this? Kenny's mom thinks Ms. Sunshine is just a regular singer at the start. But after the party, Kenny is like this brand-new kid. He listens to his mom. His grades go up."

"So Kenny was a bad egg before this?"

"Yeah, I'd have to establish that early on. But anyway, after a while the spell or whatever wears off and Kenny starts to misbehave again. His mom can't go back to the way things used to be. She wants Ms. Sunshine to sing her song again. Only Ms. Sunshine knows how much Kenny's mom wants her services now, so she charges her a lot more money than before."

Ms. Sunshine started singing about the difference between "forever friends" and "five-minute friends" who leave you at the first sign of trouble. Alex looked down at the table, glad that Yasmin was too focused on their conversation to listen to the lyrics.

"Who's the main character in this story?" she asked. "Kenny or his mom?"

Alex's first reaction was Kenny, but his mom seemed to be the one driving the story forward. Kenny was too passive to be a protagonist.

"His mom, I guess," Alex said. "I don't usually write from a grown-up's point of view, though."

"Maybe trying something new is exactly what you need."

"That sounds risky. What if I completely blow it? If we want to keep Natacha happy, the story needs to be good."

"Does it? These flowers grow from imagination and creativity, right? So why does the quality of the story matter?"

"Because it's all tied together," Alex said. "It doesn't matter how creative a story is if it's poorly told. The only way a reader will buy into all those wild ideas is if they're transported into a world where those ideas can actually happen. That takes characterization, dialogue, description, pacing . . ."

"Good writing."

"Exactly."

Ms. Sunshine was replaced by a balloon artist. He was younger than the other entertainers and wearing a diamond stud in one ear. After pumping a purple balloon into a long tube, he began to fashion it into a poodle.

"What about a balloon animal that comes to life?" Alex

asked. "I don't think that's ever been done before."

"There's never been a story about a killer corn dog, either."

"Huh?"

"Just because something's never been done before doesn't make it a good idea. Balloon animals are silly, not scary. Besides, a monster that can be defeated by a sharp pencil isn't exactly intimidating."

They batted around a few more possibilities, but nothing seemed good enough. Eventually the balloon artist was replaced by a ventriloquist holding a dummy in a tuxedo. Alex tried to think of an original idea and came up empty.

"Forget the story for now," he said. "Let's focus on our escape plan. Any ideas?"

Yasmin gave a hesitant nod. "I've been thinking about something. It's not a full-fledged plan yet, but it has possibilities."

"Hit me with it."

Yasmin turned in her chair to face him. She kept her voice low, just in case Natacha was somehow able to eavesdrop on their conversation.

"Remember how I almost pushed Natacha into that grave world?" Yasmin asked. "Trying to sneak up on her is too risky, like you said, but what if we set a trap instead?"

Yasmin explained how it would work. Alex pointed out a few flaws, and they refined the plan together. It wasn't perfect, and it would take some time to collect everything they needed, but at least they would be doing *something*. Alex was tired of being a passive character in his own story.

"I guess the first step is gathering supplies, then," Yasmin said. "The tools should be easy enough to find, but I'm not sure what we're going to use as a tarp. Even if we find something that works, sneaking it past Natacha and Simeon is going to be hard."

"Maybe we don't need a tarp," Alex said, tugging on the tablecloth. It was cloth, not vinyl, which made it strong enough to suit their needs. Besides, he liked the picture emblazoned across its surface: Frisbee Man laying waste to an army of cyborgs with one epic throw of his Flying Disc of Doom.

Yasmin laughed with delight. "Frisbee Man to the rescue! I love it!" As they folded up the tablecloth, she added, "The tricky part is going to be hiding everything once we get back to the graveyard. If one of us wanders off, they're bound to notice. We're definitely going to need help for that part." Her eyes scanned the backyard. "Lenore! You can come out now. I know you're there!"

Alex winced. "Sorry. I wanted to tell you."

"It's okay."

"How'd you figure it out?"

"Oh, I'm a regular Sherlock Holmes." Yasmin nodded toward the birthday cake, which was missing a huge chunk. "I've been watching it slowly disappear one cat-sized bite at a time."

Alex laughed, relieved he didn't have to lie anymore. "Lenore! The jig is up!"

The cat appeared, her front paws and mouth covered with blue icing, and joined them at the table. She refused to meet Yasmin's eyes. The message was clear. Even though they might be on the same team again, they were certainly not friends. Nevertheless, Alex couldn't stop smiling. At long last, they were all together again.

"You two find what we need," he said. "I think I finally have a good idea for this story."

"The singer?" Yasmin asked.

Alex shook his head.

"The magician?"

"Nope."

"The balloon guy?"

Alex laughed. "You'll just have to read it to find out."

"I'm sure it'll be worth the wait," Yasmin said.

She headed toward the gate, crossing paths with the latest entertainer to enter the backyard: a tall clown wearing suspenders. The white and red colors staining her skin did not look like makeup. Alex imagined a baby born with the face of a clown and felt a shiver run down his spine. What would *that* life be like?

"Alex!" Yasmin screamed. "No clowns! You promised!"

"Sorry!"

Yasmin squeezed past the clown and out the front gate. Lenore followed with an amused expression on her face. The clown waited a moment or two, then snuck up to the fence and tooted a long horn in Yasmin's direction. Alex heard her scream.

He opened the gravebook and started to write. By the time he finished, Yasmin had completed her inspection of the grave world. It was smaller than the others, and she hadn't been able to find any of the supplies they needed. Alex was a little disappointed, but he didn't want to be greedy. The tablecloth was a good start.

Once they were all together, he wrote the final word of the story and the world instantly began to dismantle itself. He felt a little guilty watching Kenny and his guests vanish through the tear in the sky. They might not be real, but they were still his responsibility.

The story was waiting for them on the tombstone. As Natacha read, Alex blocked her view from a carefully folded tablecloth that seemed to be moving of its own accord.

Lenore will find a good hiding place, Alex thought. *Now all we have to do is track down the other things we need.*

It felt good to have a plan, but it would only work if his stories did their job. Alex nervously waited to see what kind of flower this one would create.

THE FIFTH MACHETE

The old juggler slowly scaled the steps of the mansion and announced his presence with three taps of the brass knocker. A butler opened the door. He gave the juggler a dubious look, no doubt expecting a younger man, and ushered him into a backyard hidden from outside view by tall stone walls.

The children were waiting for him.

The juggler had been warned that his audience was "unusual," but this was a staggering understatement. They weren't even human. Many had horns and tails, but the juggler also spotted wings, maws, tentacles, scales, and a solitary pair of antennae. On each head was a cone-shaped birthday hat.

Most people would have turned and run, but the old juggler was a true professional and swallowed his fear; he had been paid to do a job, and he was going to do it. He stepped onto the wooden platform erected in the center of the backyard, gave his audience a courteous bow, and held up a single finger so they understood he would need a few moments to prepare. Even during his best years, when the juggler's shows had filled entire arenas, he had never spoken to his audience. His craft was his voice.

As the juggler opened his case and began to arrange his

props, the butler followed him onto the stage.

"I'm sorry we didn't tell you the truth," he said. "You never would have come."

"What are they?" whispered the juggler.

"The most demanding audience you'll ever face. So make sure you give the show of your life. I don't want you to end up like the magician last year."

"What happened?"

"They ate him. To be fair, he wasn't very good. At magic, that is. I can't attest to his culinary value."

The juggler's left hand began to tremble, as it sometimes did, knocking over one of the juggling pins he had placed on the stage. He reminded himself that he had once performed for kings and queens. But that was long ago, so long ago, and his reflexes weren't what they used to be. . . .

The butler squeezed the juggler's shoulder.

"I'll save you a piece of cake. It's imported from Italy. I hope you get to try it."

The butler left the stage and attempted to calm the restless audience. After hurriedly setting up his record player, the juggler placed his trusted vinyl recording of Vivaldi's "Four Seasons" onto the turntable and lowered the needle. The familiar notes calmed his racing heart.

He picked up the multicolored balls and began his routine.

These opening minutes were little more than a warm-up to loosen his limbs for the more challenging tricks to come, like stretching before going for a run. When he was younger, he could have kept the balls circling through the air with his eyes closed, but now even such a simple task required all his concentration. Nevertheless, his performance was flawless, and by the time he switched to rings, the juggler had begun to feel like his old self. He risked a quick glance at the audience and was pleased to see the wonder in their eyes. One boy was even clapping along to the music with his claws.

For the next few minutes, all was well.

Then the juggler dropped a ring.

It was his disobedient left hand again, jerking unexpectantly. A girl with a tulip growing from the top of her head retrieved the ring and handed it to him with a smile, and the juggler gave her a gallant bow. He knew from past experience that the audience would allow you a single mistake. It wasn't the end of the world.

He could still do this.

The juggler put the rings aside and picked up the juggling pins. He had just begun to regain his rhythm when he misjudged a rotation and a pin clattered to the floor. This time there was no forgiveness in the children's eyes. Less than a minute later, he dropped another pin. Then another. The juggler's palms began to grow sweaty, a fatal development. He wiped them on his pants before tossing the pins into the air, but one slipped out of his hand and landed several feet behind him.

The audience howled with laughter and crept closer to the

stage. A boy with protruding fangs and a button that said I'M EIGHT YEARS OLD TODAY! stared up at him with hungry eyes.

The juggler remembered what had happened to the magician and was suddenly very afraid.

He needed to win them over again. Now.

There was only one thing he could do.

He reached into his case and withdrew the four machetes that had always been a surefire showstopper. Knife throwing on its own wasn't so impressive, but all the other jugglers he had ever met used dulled blades. Not him. His machetes had been sharpened to a deadly edge. He demonstrated for the children by pulling an apple from his pocket and slicing it in half with a well-struck blow.

The kids cheered and returned to their original seats. They were his again, at least for now. The juggler lifted the needle from the record. For this to work, he needed complete silence.

He juggled.

It had been many years since he'd risked using the machetes; he still bore a scar along his palm from his last ill-fated attempt. No matter. It wasn't the sort of thing you forgot. The machetes whistled through the air and returned to his palm at tremendous speed, each blade more than capable of cutting through skin and bone. He prayed his left hand continued to obey him. If it trembled even the slightest bit, there was a good chance he would never juggle again.

At last, he was done.

The juggler smiled at the children, ready to take his final bow, but he could tell they weren't yet satisfied. The birthday boy snarled with displeasure and approached the stage. The other guests followed his lead, gnashing their teeth in anticipation of an early meal. Even the girl who had retrieved the juggler's ring joined the procession. As she approached, the tulip growing out of her head sprouted black thorns.

The butler had been right. This was a demanding audience. In order to survive, the juggler needed to do something truly extraordinary.

He returned to his case and withdrew the fifth machete.

This level of difficulty was a challenge even at the peak of his talents, and the juggler felt beads of sweat roll down his temples. He threw the machetes so high that sunlight glistened off their spinning blades, and the children began to clap in rhythm. The juggler barely heard them. In his mind, he was beneath the spotlights of a gilded opera house in Paris, his name in lights, the toast of the town once more, his hands a blur of motion, his fingers young and nimble. And then he gave the machetes one final toss and raised his hands triumphantly into the air as the deadly blades whistled to earth and embedded themselves in the wooden stage, forming a perfect circle around him.

The audience erupted in applause, and the juggler took a well-deserved bow. He noticed a thin trail of blood along the back of his left hand; that final throw had been just a hair off. It was a small price to pay for the most rousing success of his career.

After an excellent piece of cake and some hearty congratulations, the juggler drove home. The next morning, there was a wrapped box sitting on his front stoop. It was heavy. He brought it into the house and read the attached note.

> My daughter can't stop talking about your performance at Kenny's birthday party. She is turning nine next week and you MUST come. Won't take no for an answer. Of course, will need you to change things up to make her day SPECIAL.

The juggler opened the box. The machetes lined up inside had gilded hilts and finely sharpened blades.
All six of them.

When the flower first appeared, Alex was worried. It was unusual that the three rosebuds—red, blue, and yellow— branched off from a single stem, but other than that they were totally ordinary. Natacha looked like she was ready to voice her disappointment when the rosebuds suddenly took flight and arced through the air, magically leaping from one part of the stem to the other.

Simeon sniffed the juggling flower and gave a single, encouraging wag of his tail.

"Now that's the storyteller I know," Natacha said, and Alex couldn't help but smile.

10

GARAGE SALE

By the end of the week, Yasmin and Alex had found every-thing they needed to trap their captors, but it was proving difficult to prepare for the execution of their plan. Nata-cha and Simeon were always hovering nearby, watching their every move. Finally, the kids decided to divide and conquer. They entered the new grave worlds together, as always, but after some time had passed, Yasmin snuck back into the graveyard on her own. While Lenore stood guard, she used their secret stash to make all the necessary preparations for their trap.

At long last, they were ready.

The grave world that night was a generic suburban street. Alex and Yasmin walked past cookie-cutter houses until they reached a blue ranch at the end of a cul-de-sac. A handwritten sign on the front lawn read GARAGE SALE. Plastic tables piled with someone else's junk had been set up in the driveway. There were no customers.

"Do you remember anything about this idea?" Yasmin asked.

"I actually do," Alex replied. He picked up a pink piggy bank and inspected the piece of masking tape affixed to its nose: $1.00. "My parents spend a few weekends every year garage-sale hopping. I always come along, just in case there are any books. At one point, it occurred to me that a garage sale is the perfect way to get rid of a cursed object."

"Why not just throw it out?"

"That's part of the curse. You need to sell it to a new owner or be stuck with it forever."

"Wacky curses and their rules," Yasmin said. She waved a hand over the items on display. "So which one is it?"

Alex scratched his head. "Well . . . um . . ."

"You don't know, do you?"

"Not yet. But I know someone's going to buy it. And something creepy is going to happen when they bring it home."

"And . . ."

Alex shrugged. "And now you know as much about this story as I do."

"So we're shopping for a cursed object. Cool."

After a quick search of the first table, Yasmin suggested

an old-fashioned Ouija board. Alex shook his head. "The first word that planchette would spell out is *cliché.*"

"How about this toaster, then?"

"What's the curse? Burnt bread?"

"Jigsaw puzzle?"

That one gave Alex pause. "Maybe."

"Teddy bear?"

"I already wrote a story about one of those."

"Egg timer?"

"Another maybe."

Yasmin lifted a Raggedy Ann doll by one foot. "Come on. Creepy dolls never go out of style."

"I can't argue with that. But I just read 'Prey,' by Richard Matheson, so I'm feeling a little intimidated on the creepy doll front right now. That was such a great story."

"Write a better one."

"Yeah, right."

"Why not?" Yasmin asked.

"Because I *can't.* Even if I practiced for a hundred years, I'd never write anything as good as Richard Matheson. I just don't have it in me."

"That's not true."

"I was flipping through my old nightbooks yesterday, looking for notes on some of these abandoned ideas. I couldn't believe how many stories I had written. Sometimes two or three in a single day! It was so easy back then. Just come up with an idea and *write*."

"What changed?" Yasmin asked. "I know you mentioned things were different after the apartment, but that
doesn't make sense to me. If anything, what happened to
us proves what an awesome writer you are."

Alex was suddenly filled with a sense of deep forebod-
ing—like if he didn't share the truth with Yasmin right
now, he might not ever get the chance again.

"It's not what happened in the apartment," he said.
"It's what happened after. I was feeling confident when
we returned. I mean, my stories had been good enough to
captivate a witch! For the first time in my life, I couldn't
wait to share my writing with other people. Things will be
different now, I thought. Everyone will see how talented I
am. Only guess what? No one cared. My LA teacher? Anything I wrote was just another paper to grade. The kids at
school? Whenever I read something in front of the class,
I could see them zoning out. I tried posting a few stories
on this fiction writing forum, hoping to get some feedback
from other writers. No one read them. My family . . ." Alex
shrugged. "They love me. They really do. They're just not
book people."

Alex picked up a butterfly yo-yo and turned it in his
hands. Fifty cents. If he had gone to this garage sale with
his parents, he might have bought it.

"I started wondering what I was doing wrong," Alex

continued. "Had I lost my touch? I tried different styles, different genres. Nothing seemed to work. Writing became harder. Stories fell apart before I could finish them. Every word felt wrong. I couldn't string more than a few sentences together without wanting to erase them and start over again."

"Why didn't you tell me?" Yasmin asked.

"You were going through your own stuff," Alex said, flicking the yo-yo up and down. "And then you weren't there anymore."

"I'm sorry."

"You don't have to apologize. It's not your fault. You wanted your old life back. I get it. But if this plan works, and things go back to normal—I hope we can stay friends this time."

Yasmin nodded without meeting his eyes. Alex had gotten very good at translating body language through all his time spent with Lenore, and he understood Yasmin's response as surely as if she had spoken the words aloud: *I wish we could stay friends, but we both know that's not in the cards.*

"Do we have a winner?" Yasmin asked, nodding toward the yo-yo in his hands.

"Huh?" Alex asked, not understanding at first. "Oh. A cursed yo-yo? Nah. Even I know that's a terrible idea." He started up the front steps, shoulders slumped. "I better start writing. I'll let you know when I'm done."

"We haven't figured out an idea yet! Don't you want my help?"

"It's okay. You can't help me forever."

Before Yasmin could respond, Alex stepped inside the house and closed the door behind him.

Unlike their last few trips to the dream graveyard, Yasmin didn't have any tools to find or traps to set. That wasn't necessarily a good thing. Her mind, given time to wander, began to dwell on all the possible things that could go wrong with their plan. She wondered if they were rushing things. There was still so much they didn't understand. How was Natacha alive again? What were the flowers for?

If they failed to escape, Natacha would definitely punish them in some terrible way.

Was it worth the risk when the possible consequences were so dire?

Hoping some physical activity would clear her head, Yasmin borrowed a pink bike ($25) from the garage sale and pumped the pedals like mad. Within a few minutes, she was breathing hard, which didn't make any sense—she was currently asleep in her bed right now and not physically moving. Yasmin just went with it. If she started listing things that confused her about this entire scenario, she'd end up filling more pages than Alex. She passed the coffin and continued down the street until she hit another one of those treadmill spots that marked the edge of the grave world, then spun around and repeated the journey all over again.

The entire time, Alex's words echoed in her head: *"I hope we can stay friends this time."*

Given everything they had gone through together, and how Alex had—time and time again—proven himself worthy of her friendship, there was only one correct response: *"Of course* we'll stay friends!" That's what any decent person would have said.

Instead, she hadn't even *spoken*.

Yasmin had seen the disappointment in Alex's eyes and hated herself for it. But it would have been even crueler to give him false hope. In Yasmin's mind, her friendship with Alex and the possibility of a normal life had become flip sides of a coin. She had to choose one or the other.

Alex or a life without fear. Alex or survival.

She remembered how it had been during those dark days after the apartment. It had felt like she was fading away, becoming a ghost without the common courtesy of dying. Sometimes Yasmin would stare at herself in the mirror and state her name, half expecting her reflection to disagree.

She couldn't go back to those days again. The fear

would gnaw at her until she was just a shell of herself, an empty Yasmin.

"I'm sorry, Alex," she said.

Yasmin did a few more circles of the street and returned to the house. She killed some time building a Lego set ($30) until Alex came out and told her he was done. They walked back to the coffin in silence. Once they were standing in front of the opening, Alex wrote the final sentence of his story and the gravebook burst into flames.

By the time the world began to destroy itself, they were already back in the graveyard. As Natacha read the new story, Yasmin replaced the coffin lid and waited for the grave dirt to replenish itself. Once this new flower bloomed, they would finally put their plan into action.

Yasmin hoped they weren't making a terrible mistake.

THE WRONG PUZZLE

My grandpa is cuckoo for garage sales. He hits at least a dozen of them every weekend, then brings his "favorite granddaughter" (i.e., only granddaughter, i.e., Madison, i.e., me) these weird presents. A snow globe of Wichita, Kansas. Volume 4 of the 1989 edition of *Encyclopedia Britannica* (Delusion—Frenssen). A pair of mismatched ice skates—one too big, the other too small.

This week's present was a jigsaw puzzle.

Good news! I actually like jigsaw puzzles (unlike, say, the half-filled bottle of hot sauce that Grandpa brought me two weeks ago). I mean, they're not my first choice of entertainment, but there's something kinda Zen about tracking down just the right piece. The box of this particular jigsaw puzzle featured an adorable kitten on a flying carpet, which was so incredibly cheesy that it crossed the line into cool. (Plus, it had cost Grandpa a whopping 25 CENTS—again, favorite granddaughter.) There were only three hundred pieces, so I cleared my desk and set it up there, thinking I'd have plenty of room. Besides, it would give me a good excuse if I forgot to do my homework. ("Sorry, Ms. Ng. I really wanted to write my literary analysis of *Tuck Everlasting*, but there was a jigsaw puzzle in the way. Please accept this snow globe as a worthy substitute.")

It wasn't long before I noticed something was wrong.

So, the way I do jigsaw puzzles is to pick out the frame pieces first. (Nothing earth-shattering there. It's not like this is Madison's TOTALLY UNIQUE PRIZEWINNING METHOD. It's Jigsaw 101.) I sorted the piles into those with an edge and wannabes who would have to wait their turn—so far, so good—and then began to assemble the frame. This was where things got weird. I checked the box, and sure enough, the sky surrounding feline Aladdin was an unrealistic shade of blue. The frame pieces should have matched. Instead, they were an odd hodgepodge of colors, mostly light gray and white.

I laughed. Someone had put the wrong puzzle in the box. And after Grandpa spent an entire quarter on it, too!

I almost stopped right there and then, but it was kind of mysterious not knowing the final product, and my curiosity got the best of me. With no picture to guide me, assembling the pieces was a lot harder, but eventually I managed to finish the frame. After adding a few interior pieces, I realized I had it upside down. The white part was on the top. The gray part was at the bottom.

Ceiling. Carpet.

It was a room of some sort. Interesting.

I grabbed a snack and rolled my sleeves up. Within twenty minutes, I had made more progress than I expected. Usually when I do jigsaw puzzles, there's a ton of trial and error, but luck was with me that day. Most times, I was able to fit the piece into the right spot on the first try.

It was like the puzzle wanted to be put together.

In no time at all, the ceiling and carpet were completed. I moved on to the rest of the room. Soon I had half a bookshelf, the legs of a bed, what might have been a stuffed animal. . . .

When I turned over a piece revealing a giant wooden *D*, I nearly fell out of my seat. An identical *D* was hanging on the wall above my desk, part of the whole M-A-D-I-S-O-N collection.

I dropped the puzzle piece.

This was *my* room.

I won't lie. I kinda freaked. I ran downstairs to tell my parents, but they were at my brother's Little League game. The house was totally quiet. I decided to hang out in the living room and watch TV. There was no way I was going back into my bedroom alone.

And then it hit me.

"Grandpa," I said, smacking myself with a well-deserved facepalm.

My grandfather is known for two things. The first, as established, is his love of garage sales. But he is also a hard-core practical joker. I'm talking everything from flies in ice cubes to slipping a fake traffic ticket underneath my dad's windshield wiper. It was a piece of cake to order a personalized jigsaw puzzle online—all you needed was a photograph. Grandpa must have snapped a pic of my room, had the puzzle made, and then switched it out with the one from the garage sale.

"Well played, Grandpa," I said, impressed.

I started to text him, then got a better idea. After a quick phone search, I found the flying cat puzzle on Amazon and used the remaining balance of an old gift card to order it. After I put it together, I would show Grandpa the cat puzzle and pretend it was the one he had gotten me from the garage sale. He would be so confused!

Ha! Grandpa wasn't the only practical joker in the family!

Now that I knew the score, I wasn't freaked out anymore. I went upstairs and returned to the puzzle, figuring I might as well finish it. I pieced together my bookshelves, my posters, even my schoolbag in the corner. As I assembled my desk, I noticed that I was actually in the puzzle, sitting in my chair and working on something. Grandpa must have snuck up on me while I was doing my homework. In fact, I could see his shadow stretched across the carpet. Or, at least, a shadow. It wasn't Grandpa. He was a tall man, and this shadow was the size of a child.

He must have gotten my brother to take the picture, I thought, a perfectly reasonable explanation. Still, I found myself listening for the sound of my family's return. Grandpa might even be with them. I could ask him if he had really switched out the puzzle, or . . .

"Or what?" I asked. "The puzzle he bought at the garage sale was of my room? That's impossible."

I decided to finish the thing before my imagination got out of hand. There were only a few pieces remaining. A spot in the wall just to the left of the bookshelf. A pair of sneakers peeking out from under my bed.

The last piece was the section of carpet just above my brother's shadow.

Except it wasn't just carpet.

"What is that?" I asked, squinting my eyes for a closer look.

As far as I could tell, my brother was wearing a weird sort of hat. It looked like the cap jokers wear on a playing card, with three different sections that stuck up and then flopped over. I could even see the bells dangling from the ends.

My brother didn't own anything like that.

And just like that, I knew this wasn't a practical joke. The puzzle in front of me was the one my grandpa had bought. I figured it changed based on who was putting it together. I had no idea why someone would sell it at a garage sale. Maybe it had been an accident. Or maybe they had wanted the puzzle out of their house, so they had slipped it into an innocent-looking box and sold it for a quarter.

Break it apart, shouted a frantic voice in my head. *Now! Before it's too late!*

I tried, but it was no use; my fingertips glided over the surface. The lines between the pieces had faded away. What remained was no longer a puzzle at all. By completing it, I had somehow made it whole.

I stared down at this perfect replica of my room and realized that something had changed.

The shadow was gone.

Behind me, I heard my bedroom door squeak open, followed by the tinkling of bells.

Yasmin got down on her knees and watched the new stem emerge from the grave soil. She thought Alex had really hit the bull's-eye this time, so she was expecting something special.

When the flower finished blooming, however, it was about as ordinary as you could get.

"What is *that*?" Natacha asked.

"It looks like a tulip," said Yasmin.

"I know it's a tulip!" Natacha exclaimed. "A boring tulip that you can find at any florist in the world."

"I don't understand," Alex stammered. "That was a good story! At least, I think it was a good story. Maybe I should have—"

Yasmin leaped to his defense. "It was an *amazing* story—and original! Something's wrong. That should have made a spectacular flower."

"Well, it didn't," said Natacha, crossing her arms. "So you need to write me another one before I let you wake up again."

"No way," Yasmin said.

"I'm sorry—do you think you have a choice? Forget one story. Now I want three. And if it takes you a month, so be it. I have all the time in the world."

Simeon yipped, getting their attention, and swatted the tulip with his paw. It broke into a dozen parts. Yasmin picked one up and turned it over in her hands.

It was a puzzle piece.

Yasmin gave Natacha a triumphant smile.

"Unique enough for you?" she asked.

"No one likes a gloater," replied Natacha. "Don't just stand there and gawk. Put it back together!"

Yasmin knelt down and picked up a piece. One side was bright yellow, like the tulip, but the other side was fuzzy and green. Together, the kids built a new flower with the fuzzy side out. When it was done, it looked more like a lily than a tulip, with three drooping petals that ended in tiny bells. Natacha tapped one with her finger. The bell rang, and an ominous *dong* reverberated throughout the graveyard. Yasmin clapped her hands over her ears.

Simeon sniffed this new flower and yipped in delight.

"That's better," Natacha said. "Still—I feel like you missed a golden opportunity. You left out the ending! I assume your demonic jester did something *awful* to that girl"—her eyes glowed at the prospect—"but it's no fair keeping it a secret after I forced myself to read the entire story."

"Sometimes it's better to leave it to the imagination," Alex said, straightening his glasses. Yasmin was glad to see him stand his ground. At this moment, at least, he looked a little more like his old self.

"You expect me to figure it out *myself*?" Natacha asked.

"That sounds exhausting. Just tell me what really happened."

"Nothing *really* happened. It's a story."

"Fine," Natacha said, placing her hands on her hips. "The girl got trapped in the puzzle. She took the jester's place. That's what you were thinking, right?"

Alex refused to answer, which only infuriated Natacha more.

"The jester was just her brother all dressed up," the witch said. "It was a practical joke after all."

Alex shrugged.

Natacha smiled knowingly. "I've got it! The jester cut the girl into puzzle pieces!"

"Eww," Yasmin said. Even Alex looked a little grossed out.

"What . . . happened . . . then?" Natacha asked, spitting out each word between gritted teeth.

"That's on a need-to-know basis," Alex said. "And you don't need to know."

Natacha gasped, floored by this unexpected impertinence. She leaned over them, danger in her eyes.

At that moment, Lenore dashed between the witch's legs.

Natacha stumbled and fell.

"How did that *cat* get in here?" she shrieked, slamming her fists against the ground. "Simeon! Get her!"

The jackal took off in hot pursuit, and Lenore led him deeper into the graveyard. Her job was to keep Simeon busy so he couldn't protect Natacha during the next phase of their plan. Within moments, both animals were out of sight.

Stay safe, Yasmin thought.

"I've always hated that cat," Natacha grumbled, starting to rise. "She was only ever loyal to Griselda, plus she left hair *everywhere. . . .*"

Yasmin yanked the lily out of the earth. The motion caused all three bells to ring, producing an unearthly peal.

"Put. That. Down," Natacha snarled.

Yasmin sprinted in one direction, Alex in another, forcing Natacha to choose which of them to pursue. *Pick me*, Yasmin thought, shaking the lily so it rang even louder. Alex wasn't exactly a speedster, and there was a chance Natacha might catch him. If that happened, their plan was dead on arrival.

Natacha took the bait, and the chase was on.

There was nowhere to hide, no tricks to pull. Yasmin focused on her footing, dodging tombstones, leaping over loose dirt. She was faster than the witch, but that advantage could be undone by a single misplaced step. Magic was the other variable. At any moment, Yasmin expected a lightning flash to strike her to the ground, or a paralysis spell to freeze her limbs in midstride.

At last, they came to the tombstone engraved with a clock. Yasmin had chosen this particular grave because it sat next to a crumbling tablet overgrown with tall grass, which had provided her with an ideal hiding spot for the objects she would desperately need in just a few minutes.

Yasmin leaped over the freshly tilled dirt and tumbled to the ground as though she had landed wrong. She grasped her ankle and moaned in apparent pain.

Natacha slowed to a walk.

"Oh dear," she said as she approached the grave, "looks like someone's hurt herself."

Yasmin tried to look as defenseless as possible, a prey with nowhere else to go. *Just another few steps.* "Do you even know what my name is?" she asked.

Natacha thought about it. "Jessica?"

"You ruined my life, and you don't even know my name."

"*I* ruined *your* life? My life was perfect until you and Story Boy showed up. I had a great apartment. A booming business. All the magic I could ever want. Oh—you know what else? I was *alive*. So if anyone deserves some sympathy here, it's—"

Natacha stepped onto the grave.

She had no reason to expect anything other than solid earth beneath her feet. What Natacha didn't know, of course, was that Yasmin had made some modifications. First, she had dug up the coffin and raised it a good two feet so it was nearly flush with the ground. After that, she had replaced the wooden lid with the Frisbee Man tablecloth they had stolen from Kenny's party, pulling it as taut as possible. Finally, Yasmin had refilled the dirt to the sides of the coffin and sprinkled a thin layer on top of the tablecloth—just enough to conceal it.

Natacha wasn't stepping on packed dirt. In fact, the only thing supporting her weight was a cheap piece of cloth.

She plummeted straight through.

Knowing there wasn't a moment to waste, Yasmin sprang to her feet and dragged the coffin lid from its hiding spot in the grass. Before lowering it into place, she took a quick glance into the grave world. Natacha was trapped inside a giant clock. The witch was trying to crawl back to the graveyard, but the hem of her dress was caught between two shifting gears as large as carousel platforms.

"Girl!" Natacha shrieked. "Let me out of here right now!"

"My name's Yasmin."

She dropped the lid into place and climbed on top of it, adding some weight; it wouldn't be long before Natacha tore free of the gears and tried to escape. Luckily, Alex had finally caught up. He was gasping for breath.

"Is she . . . ? Did you . . . ?"

"Get over here!" Yasmin exclaimed. Alex leaped onto the coffin, adding his weight just as Natacha slammed into the barrier from the other side. Yasmin felt the lid rise an inch or two before falling into place again.

"The coffin's upright from her perspective," Alex said. "That means she can get a running start. We have to hurry."

"Stay here," Yasmin said. She retrieved two hammers and a coffee can full of nails from the tall grass, returning just as Natacha plowed into the lid a second time and knocked it askew. Yasmin saw the witch's fingers claw for purchase through the narrow opening and struck them with the hammer, producing a scream of agony from the other side.

The hand withdrew.

Yasmin straightened the lid and pounded the first nail into place. Alex grabbed the second hammer and they worked together, using their weight to hold the lid down while they secured it with as many of the long steel nails as possible. Natacha's attacks gradually lessened in intensity and then stopped altogether.

"I think that's enough," Alex said.

Yasmin, breathing hard, saw that the lid was covered with nail heads. She lowered her hammer. Natacha wasn't going anywhere.

"Finish the story," Yasmin said.

"You sure? Trapping her might be enough."

"No way. We need to end this, once and for all."

Alex gave a hesitant nod and retrieved the last item hidden in the tall grass. It was the gravebook that had appeared when Yasmin first opened the coffin. She had brought it to Alex, along with a description of what she had seen in the clock world, and he had gradually added a story—leaving out the final word. They hadn't wanted to spring their trap too early.

"You're making a mistake," Natacha said.

Her voice was garbled and distant, as though they were speaking over a bad phone connection. It was more than just a thin piece of wood separating them. The witch was an entire world away. Nevertheless, Yasmin could hear the desperation in her voice. No matter how much Yasmin hated Natacha, it made her feel a little bad.

Alex found the right spot in the gravebook and raised his pen. "Are we doing the right thing?" he asked.

Yasmin nodded. "What's the last word?" she asked.

"'Them.' Never thought a boring old pronoun could be so dangerous."

He scribbled the word and dropped the book. It burst into blue flame. A few moments later, the coffin began to shake and rattle. Yasmin expected Natacha to scream and beg for help.

She started to laugh instead.

"You *fools*," she said. "You can't wake up on your own, remember? If you kill me, you'll be trapped here forever!"

"You're lying," Alex said, bending down next to the coffin. "Once you're gone, all your spells will stop working, just like with Aunt Gris and the apartment. That's how magic works."

Natacha laughed even harder.

"Do you really think . . . this has anything to do . . . with magic?" she asked. "My death accomplishes nothing! He's the only one who can set you free!"

Alex and Yasmin shared a perplexed look. "He?" they asked in unison.

Yasmin heard movement and saw Simeon approaching the grave. He was carrying Lenore in his mouth like a dead rabbit. She wasn't moving. The jackal dropped her and seemed to read the entire situation with his luminous gray eyes: the kids, the coffin, the missing witch. Yasmin tensed, expecting the animal to attack, but instead Simeon gave a long sigh and took a seat in the grass.

He began to change.

This wasn't a painful transformation like in the old werewolf movie Alex had forced her to watch. There was no breaking and re-forming of bones, no screams of torment. Simeon was simply a jackal one moment and a boy the next. It looked about as difficult as unfolding a beach towel.

"I thought it was about time we talked in person," he said.

II

THE NÄCHPYR

Alex stared at the boy in disbelief. He was about ten years old and looked like he belonged in a hospital bed. His skin was sallow, his arms as thin as matchsticks, his face gaunt. There was something wrong with his left ear. It was twice the normal size, with a curtain of thin, reddish skin covering the canal. Indeed, the only thing that looked remotely healthy about the tiny figure was his luxurious blond hair. Alex suspected the boy—or whatever he was—took a certain pride in this. The hair was carefully parted to one side, leaving a perfect sliver of scalp.

"Who are you?" Yasmin asked as Alex ran to Lenore's side. Her breathing was weak, but she was still alive. He placed a comforting hand on her chest, just to let her know he was there.

"You might as well call me Simeon," the boy said. "It's

a name I've used before."

"*What* are you?" Alex asked.

Simeon looked at them with cold amusement. His slate-gray eyes were not the eyes of a child.

"That's a longer story. I should rescue my witch first."

He started toward the coffin. The lid was rattling like a storm door during a tornado. Alex wondered if Natacha was even there anymore. The hole in the sky might have already swallowed her.

Yasmin, however, wasn't taking any chances. She stepped in front of Simeon, blocking his path.

"You're not helping her," she said.

Simeon chuckled and tapped her shoulder. Yasmin screamed and began frantically swatting at her body.

"Get them off me!" she exclaimed, her eyes bulging with fear. "They're everywhere!"

"There's nothing there," Alex said. "It's some kind of trick."

"One of them just crawled up my nose!"

Yasmin pinched her fingers together and shoved them up her nostril. She yanked hard and made a flinging motion toward the grass. For just a moment, Alex thought he saw something long and brown wiggle into the dirt.

A worm, Alex thought. *That can't be a coincidence.*

Yasmin hated worms. No particular reason. They just grossed her out. Simeon had somehow identified that fear and was using it against her. As Alex tried to explain this to his friend, however, there was an explosion behind him, and a coffin lid landed a few yards to his left.

He turned around and saw Simeon helping Natacha out of the grave. Her dress was tattered, her hair in disarray.

"You!" she snarled, pointing at the kids with one trembling finger.

She marched toward them, looking as though she intended to grind their bones for soup.

"Stop," Simeon said.

Natacha didn't look happy about it, but she obeyed Simeon's command. Alex felt Yasmin's hand touch his own. She wasn't freaking out anymore, so he assumed the wormy illusions had come to a stop.

"They tried to kill me!" Natacha exclaimed, stomping her foot.

"They tried to survive," Simeon replied. "You or I would have done the same. It's your fault for being so careless."

Natacha looked like she wanted to argue, but she didn't dare. *She's scared of him*, Alex thought. It was a startling revelation.

"What *are* you?" Alex asked for the second time.

"A nachpyr."

"A *what?*"

Simeon chuckled. "For once, a monster you haven't

heard of. No surprise there. My kind excels at staying in the shadows, both literally and figuratively. You know what a vampire is, of course. Think of a nachpyr as the next step in a necessary evolution."

"You're a vampire?" Yasmin asked, her hand straying toward her neck.

Simeon was clearly offended by the suggestion. "I'm no more one of those disgusting scavengers than you are an ape. Leaving bodies in every alleyway and teeth marks on every neck—is it any wonder they were hunted to extinction? Fortunately, there was a faction of more imaginative vampires—poets, musicians, artists—who understood that the taking of a human's life force didn't have to be so messy and obvious." Simeon folded his hands behind his back like a college professor delivering a lecture, reminding Alex that he was much older than he appeared. "With the help of a coven sympathetic to our cause, we transformed our bodies so they could feed not only in a more secretive manner, but in a way that allowed us to capitalize upon our creative prowess."

"So you don't drink blood?" Alex asked.

"Of course not. My fangs were removed centuries ago." Simeon winced at the memory. "That part hurt. And before you ask, I'm perfectly capable of walking in the sun, though I don't particularly like it—I might not melt into a pile of goop like my ancestors did, but I'm prone to terrible sunburns. We did retain the more useful aspects of our former nature, however. Strength. Speed. Eternal youth. I refuse to transform into a bat—far too kitschy—but I could if I wanted to, as well as several other animals. As you've probably guessed, a jackal is my preferred form."

"If you don't drink blood, then what do you eat?" asked Alex.

Simeon's gray eyes gleamed. "Fear. More specifically, the pure, undiluted fear that only a perfect nightmare can create. In my glory days, I lived in the waking world during the day and crept into bedrooms at night, weaving the most terrifying dreams in my victims' minds and feasting on their terror. I was strong. Powerful." He clenched his teeth with frustration. "Not like now."

"What happened?" Alex asked.

Before Simeon could answer, Natacha poked his arm like a petulant child. "Um, not that your life history isn't totally fascinating, but when are we going to punish the children?"

Simeon turned on her with a look of annoyance. Natacha stiffened.

"Why don't you take care of it, *witch*?" he asked, imbuing the last word with a mocking cadence. "Come on! Dazzle us with a grand display of fearsome witchcraft! Oh, wait. You don't have a magical bone in your body, do you? In fact, all the 'spells' you've cast have been my doing. I wanted the kids to believe you could hurt them. I wanted them to be scared. But let's be honest, Natacha. You couldn't pull a rabbit out of a hat."

Natacha's cheeks turned red. "I'm the one who told you about Alex! Without me, you never would have found him at all."

"True," Simeon conceded. "And I do agree that we can't have our prisoners running amok. There must be consequences. Let's start with the cat."

Simeon reached out and Lenore floated toward him, coming to a sudden stop inches from his extended hand. Alex and Yasmin tried to intercede, but Natacha grabbed both kids and held them tight.

"Watch carefully," she whispered in their ears. "This is going to be *fun*."

"Such a majestic creature," Simeon said, circling the unconscious cat like an art lover appreciating a sculpture. "A dream walker, like me. In a different life, we could have been friends! Alas, I can't allow her to interfere with my plans."

Simeon lifted Lenore's long tail and gently blew on it from one end to the other. As he did, it burned away in a flash of magical fire.

Lenore vanished.

"What did you do to her?" Alex screamed, breaking free of Natacha's grip. Tears were flowing from his eyes.

"Relax," Simeon said. "Lenore is waiting for you in your

bedroom, safe and sound. She won't be coming back here, though. All her magic's in the tail. Now that it's gone, her dream-walking days are done."

"You monster," Yasmin said.

"Do you know the horrors I *could* have inflicted?" Simeon asked, taken aback. "Lenore can still live a long and happy life. She just won't be able to help you anymore. That wasn't the act of a monster. If anything, it was an act of kindness. Now I wonder if I did the right thing. Maybe I should have killed your precious cat. Then you would take me seriously." Simeon got close to Alex and stared into his eyes. "You think I'm weak, don't you?"

Sensing that he was treading on dangerous ground, Alex instinctively shook his head.

"You do!" Simeon exclaimed. "It's because I'm trapped here, isn't it? It's because I can't come to the waking world and slide through your bedroom window at night. You think I can't hurt you. You don't see me for what I am! You don't *fear* me."

"Perhaps an example would help," Natacha suggested. "We can't kill the boy. No boy, no flowers. But *Yasmin* here? She's a rotten apple just begging to be plucked." Natacha grinned at Alex. "How do you like that simile, storyteller?"

"It's actually a metaphor," Alex said. "You didn't use 'like' or—"

"Not now, Alex," Yasmin said between gritted teeth.

"Is the girl truly expendable?" Simeon asked. "She was brought here to help Alex compose his stories, and there's no doubt that his work has improved since her arrival."

"Not expendable," Yasmin said, raising her hand. "Definitely not expendable."

"I can't do this without her," added Alex.

"Don't listen to him," Natacha said. "He's just trying to save her. The only reason I wanted the girl here in the first place was to get our storyteller back on track. She's served her purpose. All she can do now is cause more trouble."

Simeon massaged the back of his neck while pacing back and forth. He might have looked like a fourth grader, but he had the mannerisms of an old man. The effect was disconcerting.

"I suppose you're right," he finally said. "Maybe she's more trouble than she's worth."

A long appendage emerged from the back of Simeon's neck and crooked over his head. It looked like a spinal column constructed from black bone. At its end was a bulbous, scorpion-like telson with a red stinger.

Natacha grabbed Yasmin before she could run, and Simeon started in their direction. As he approached, his spine stinger twisted and cracked like someone stretching their back. "I'll make it fast," he told Yasmin in a consoling voice. "There's no point in needlessly prolonging your fear. That'll just make me hungry, and it's not like I can eat anything in this insidious dream world. Why torment myself?"

Alex longed to stop Simeon, to save his friend, to do *something*—but all he could do was watch. Facing down a real monster was a lot different than defeating one on a page. They were *scary*. He felt betrayed by all the movies that had promised gentle, misunderstood giants or vampires with tortured souls.

Get over it, he thought. *You have to help her. Now!*

Alex stepped in front of Yasmin.

"If you hurt her," he said, speaking slowly to minimize the trembling of his voice, "you'll never get another scary story from me."

"Ha!" Natacha cackled. "Like you have a choice. You're trapped here. You have to write."

"Step aside, Alex," Simeon said.

"Oh, I'll keep writing," Alex said, "but I'm thinking those flowers you love so much grow best from the scary stuff, don't they? I mean, why else use me?"

"So what?" Natacha asked.

"You might be able to trap me here. But you can't tell me what to write. Maybe I'll change it up a little. How about an adorable koala bear who finds his way home? Or a kind grandfather who delivers nuggets of wisdom during a fishing trip with his troubled grandson? Oh, I know! A boy who doesn't fit in at school makes a special new friend!"

"Ignore him," Natacha said. "He's bluffing."

Simeon didn't look convinced. "You'd really pollute your stories with such joy?"

"You know what I've always wanted to write?" Alex asked. "A story about a little girl whose dad comes home from the war just in time for Christmas! So *heartwarming* and *inspirational*! What kind of flower do you think would grow from that one? A daffodil that gives you a hug? Or maybe a sunflower that radiates actual sunlight. One thing's for sure. You hurt Yasmin, and you'll never see the kind of flower you like again."

Simeon crossed his arms. "How can I be sure the two of you won't try to escape again?"

"Oh, we definitely will," Alex said. "It's kind of our thing. That's why you have to let her go."

"What?" Yasmin asked with an incredulous expression.

Natacha laughed. "That's not going to happen."

"I'm the one who writes the stories," Alex said. "I'm the one you need—the *only* one."

"Didn't you just tell us you couldn't do this without her?" Simeon asked.

"Natacha was right—I was just trying to save her. I'm out of my writing slump. I don't need Yasmin's help anymore."

"So she is expendable!" Natacha exclaimed. "Well, if that's the case—"

"But that doesn't change what I said. If you hurt her, I'll never help you. But let her go, and I'm yours forever. You'll be drowning in flowers."

"Absolutely not," Yasmin said. "You're not going to just stay here while—"

"This is what you wanted," Alex said. "A normal life."

"Not like this!"

"I agree to your terms," Simeon said.

"Well, I *don't*!" exclaimed Yasmin.

"Me either," said Natacha. "You're going to let her go *free*? That's not a punishment. That's a reward. You were right, you know. These kids aren't scared of you. You're like the juggler in Alex's story. A once-great performer past his prime. So take some advice from the one they actually fear. Don't be weak. You need to strike terror into this boy's heart so he knows what will happen if he ever crosses you again."

Simeon nodded. "That's good advice."

His stinger flicked past Yasmin and struck Natacha on the neck. Her mouth fell open in surprise as she collapsed to the floor.

"There," Simeon said. "Now they know what I'm capable of."

Natacha stared up at the false sky. "You promised," she whispered, a single tear rolling down her cheek. "If I helped . . . you'd bring me back. Real life . . . not this . . . dreams . . ."

Simeon knelt next to Natacha and stroked her hair. "You've played your part well. But I'm afraid you're no longer useful to me."

"You promised . . . ," Natacha said, and disappeared.

Simeon rose to his feet. The spine stinger retracted into his body and vanished.

"Death and dreams share geography," Simeon said, "and sometimes the borders overlap. I found Natacha's spirit tenaciously clinging to life, unwilling to pass over. She told me all about the marvelous stories you created for Griselda, and I knew you were the one I needed. She led me here. I owe her a debt of gratitude."

"You killed her," Yasmin said, still looking down at the spot where Natacha had fallen.

"Quickly. Painlessly. Because she was my friend. Can you imagine the torment I might inflict upon a prisoner who doesn't live up to his obligations?" His eyes hardened. "Do you fear me *now*?"

The children nodded.

"One scary story, every night, for the rest of your life," said Simeon. "Do that, and Yasmin remains free from harm."

Yasmin shook her head. "Alex, you can't."

"I agree," Alex said.

A soft rain began to fall, smearing the moon across the sky.

"It's time to go," Simeon said. "Yasmin—farewell. You will never return to this place. But let me be clear about one other thing. There is to be no contact between the two of you ever again. Not even a wave across a crowded street. I'll be watching. You break that rule, and our agreement is null and void."

Alex wiped the rain from his face and took a final look at the girl he still considered his best friend. It seemed inconceivable that he would never see her again, but if that was what it took to keep her safe, it was worth it.

Yasmin stepped toward him. There were tears in her eyes. "Could we at least have a moment to say—"

"Awake," said Simeon.

12

LENORE SHOWS HER ARTISTIC SIDE

Yasmin sat on the aluminum bleachers and watched the Little Leaguers practice. They seemed so carefree. Chewing gum. Pounding their mitts. Pretending to be the heroes they watched on TV. What bliss to worry only about curveballs and sharply hit grounders—and not dream vampires with deadly stingers.

You could be one of those carefree kids yourself, Yasmin thought. *Just forget about what happened.*

The temptation was there. Locking away the past was a learned skill, and she had gotten very, very good at it. At this point, it would be as easy as setting the parental controls on a phone. The secret was to focus on the present and not think about the past at all. If you did that for long enough, the unattended memories began to wither like a poorly watered plant.

Is that what you want? To forget about Alex completely?

What choice did she have? Simeon had been crystal clear. No contact. As long as they followed this simple rule, they would both remain safe. Despite his youthful appearance, Simeon was an ancient creature who had been born and bred during a time when things like honor still mattered. She felt like she could trust him.

I bet Natacha thought the same thing, and look how it ended for her.

It was a valid point. Yasmin wasn't going to mourn the witch, but she didn't like the idea that Simeon had killed her simply to set an example. It was the dismissive nature of it, more than the act itself, that disturbed Yasmin. What if Alex came down with an incurable case of writer's block? How long before Simeon decided he wasn't worth the trouble anymore?

Yasmin might be safe, but Alex was definitely not.

Could she really just abandon him?

The Little Leaguers started to chant—stomping their feet, laughing. It was just a silly ditty, a way to pass the time, but it tugged at Yasmin like the call of a siren.

A normal life. Forget Alex. You're safe. You're free. You're—

"Shut up," Yasmin said, covering her ears.

She heard movement behind her and saw Lenore sitting on the top row of the bleachers. The cat's once-beautiful tail was little more than a stubby, hairless knob.

"Hey, Lenore," Yasmin said, nervously scanning the park. Simeon had claimed he would be watching her at all times, but he had also said he couldn't enter the "waking world." That seemed like a contradiction. How could he see what she was doing if he was trapped in the realm of dreams?

Alex would probably know, but Alex wasn't here.

Maybe Simeon can't come here in a physical form, Yasmin thought, *but he can walk around unseen, like a ghost.* For all she knew, he might be sitting next to her right now.

She slid to the edge of the bench, just in case, and turned toward Lenore.

"How's your tail?" she asked quietly. Simeon had never expressly prohibited her from interacting with the cat, but it still made her nervous. "Does it hurt?"

Lenore gave her a scathing look: *What do you think?*

"It's too bad we're not back in the apartment. I could make some of that healing poultice for you. How about Alex? He doing okay?"

Lenore tilted her head to the side. Yasmin wasn't as good as Alex at reading the cat's expressions, but this one was unmistakable: *Do you even care?*

"Of course I care!" Yasmin exclaimed.

Lenore tilted her head a bit farther.

"What do you want me to do? I can't go into his dream anymore. Alex is on his own." Yasmin threw her face into her hands. "I am so epically over my head, Lenore. Nach-pyrs and story graveyards? It actually makes me miss witches. At least I *understood* them. I remember Alex saying—right here, actually—that in horror movies the heroes always find an expert to help them. Except this isn't a movie. It's just me, and I have no idea what to do."

Lenore leaped off the bleachers, landing with perfect grace, and darted to the edge of the ball field. After a quick check to make sure no one was looking, she used her paw fingers to etch a simple drawing in the dirt.

"A witch's hat?" Yasmin asked. "Are you trying to tell me something about Natacha? Natacha's dead."

Lenore shook her head. *Not Natacha.*

"Aunt Gris?"

No.

"Well, I don't know any other witches!"

Lenore pointed at Yasmin.

"*I'm* not a witch."

The cat covered her face with a paw and shook her head. Yasmin felt like the weak link in the world's strangest game of Pictionary. Lenore quickly added an additional drawing: a book.

"Is that a gravebook?" Yasmin asked.

No.

"Does it represent Alex?"

Another shake of the head. Lenore pointed at Yasmin

and made a writing motion with her paw.

"You want me to write something?"

No.

Yasmin kept asking questions. Finally, she figured out that the book was somehow connected to her, not Alex. But how did that make any sense? The only writing Yasmin ever did was in school.

Finally, Lenore added a third drawing that looked like a test tube and everything clicked together.

"Natacha's ledger," Yasmin said.

Back in the apartment, Yasmin had kept the books for Natacha's magic oil business. Their system was simple: the witch scribbled each order on a Post-it note, and Yasmin inputted the information into a leather-bound ledger, adding and subtracting totals when needed. She hadn't minded this job at all. Math had always come easily to her, and there was something satisfying about arranging the numbers into perfectly ordered rows and columns. Sometimes Yasmin found herself flipping through the ledger just for fun. It went back fifteen years and included the purchase history and address of all Natacha's customers. For the most part, these were just everyday people who had heard about Natacha's "special oils" through word of mouth. Yasmin had noticed, however, that there was a single customer—"Maria Goffel"—who received a sizable discount. Although Yasmin really shouldn't have cared one way or the other, the idea that this Goffel lady was throwing off her meticulous calculations grated at her. At last, she asked Natacha why such a generous discount needed to be applied.

"She's a witch like me," Natacha had said, puffing out her chest. "We got to stick together."

A witch.

They needed an expert, and it turned out that Yasmin knew exactly where to find one. She even remembered the address: 402 Tower Boulevard, Astoria.

"Have you heard of a woman named Maria Goffel?" Yasmin asked Lenore.

The cat eagerly nodded her head and pointed to the witch's hat.

"She's a witch, isn't she?"

Yes.

"You've met her?"

No. After a few more questions, Yasmin determined that Lenore had never actually seen Maria Goffel in person. Natacha, however, had talked about her all the time. That's how Lenore knew she was a witch who ordered oils on a regular basis. *Smart cat,* Yasmin thought. She still wasn't sold on the idea, though. What if Natacha and this Maria Goffel used to be friends? Going to see her might be the worst mistake Yasmin ever made.

"I don't know, Lenore. I want to help Alex, but every

witch I've ever met has tried to kill me. Seems kinda dumb to knock on one's door."

Lenore managed a shrugging gesture with what remained of her tail: *Do you have any better ideas?*

"Let me ask you a question first. You've been around a long, long time. How many *good* witches have you met?"

Lenore looked down at her paws.

"Exactly."

Nevertheless, Yasmin plugged the address into her phone, just to see if it was even possible to travel there by public transportation. There didn't seem to be a 402 Tower Boulevard, but there was a 400 and a 404, so obviously it was right in the middle. Yasmin pulled the area up on Google Maps and saw a row of small businesses on a busy street.

"Looks safe enough," she said. "Then again, so did Bayside Apartments."

The location was walkable from Queensboro Plaza. If she caught the next 7 train, she could be there in forty-five minutes.

"This is a bad idea, Lenore," Yasmin said. "We should at least sleep on it first."

Except while she was sleeping in her warm cozy bed enjoying perfectly normal dreams, Alex would be trapped in the graveyard, fighting for his life. Not checking this lead out—today, this moment, *right now*—was just another form of abandoning him.

This is it. Are you his friend or not?

Yasmin started toward the subway station, and Lenore nudged her leg with just the slightest hint of approval. The cat hadn't forgiven her completely, but at least Yasmin had taken a step in the right direction.

13

SNIP, SNAP, SNOUT

It turned out there wasn't a 402 Tower Boulevard after all.

Yasmin found 400 easily enough, a small pizzeria that promised the "best pizza in Astoria." The store next to it—404—was a dry cleaner. While it didn't promise the "cleanest clothes in Astoria," it did offer next-day service. Yasmin went into both businesses and inquired about 402. No one knew anything. To add insult to injury, the pizza was adequate at best.

"Maybe I've got the address wrong," Yasmin said, thinking hard. "Though I could have sworn—"

She was struck by the sudden sensation that someone was watching her. Yasmin scanned the pedestrians on either side of the street, but no one was remotely interested in a thirteen-year-old girl and her stubby-tailed cat.

She remembered her earlier theory about Simeon being

able to spy on her without being seen.

Stop it, Yasmin thought. *You're just being paranoid.*

Lenore suddenly took off and vanished around a corner.

"Lenore? Where are you going?"

Yasmin chased her down a narrow alleyway filled with grimy puddles. Two kids having a conversation on a fire escape watched her as she passed. The alleyway emptied into a tiny area filled with precariously balanced garbage bags. There were flies everywhere. Yasmin swatted a few away and covered her nose.

"This place is disgusting, Lenore! What are we doing here?"

Three metal doors were set into the back of a brick building. The numbers 400 and 404 had been written on the doors to the left and right. On the center door was written both a number—402—and what Yasmin assumed was the name of a store:

SNIP, SNAP, SNOUT

"So weird," Yasmin said. "Why isn't there a front entrance?"

It was also strange that the people she'd talked to at the pizza shop and dry cleaner hadn't mentioned the door when she asked them about 402. They must have known it was here—this was clearly where they took out the trash every day. And what kind of business was "Snip, Snap, Snout" anyway? Yasmin googled the words on her phone and learned that they were part of a famous expression used at the end of fairy tales: "Snip, snap, snout. This tale's told out."

"Ugh," she said. "Not fairy tales again."

She added Astoria, Queens, to "snip, snap, snout," just to see if she got any hits. Nothing. As far as the internet was concerned, 402 Tower Boulevard didn't exist.

"We came this far," Yasmin said. "Let's at least take a peek inside. You should probably turn invisible first. Most businesses don't allow pets."

Lenore did her best, but all she could manage was a ghostly dimming. She was still very much visible.

"Oh no," Yasmin said, clapping a hand to her mouth. "When Simeon cut your tail off, I think it affected all your magic, not just the dream walking."

Lenore hissed, clearly dismayed by this unexpected development.

"I'm so sorry," Yasmin said, "but it might be easier if you wait outside for now. I'll be quick, promise."

With her head hung low, Lenore found one of the few spots not covered with trash and lay down. A fly landed on her back. In the past, Lenore would have swatted it away

160

with her tail, but there was no way it could reach now.

A second fly landed. Lenore tucked her head into her chest and closed her eyes.

Yasmin stepped through the door and found herself in a small hair salon. A smocked man was sitting in a revolving barber's chair, getting his hair cut by a pleasantly plump woman wearing a Grateful Dead T-shirt. Through the storefront window, Yasmin could see traffic zipping back and forth along Tower Boulevard. She had been standing at that exact same spot just minutes ago.

That window definitely wasn't there before, Yasmin thought. *There's no way I would have missed it.*

". . . that's why you gotta homeschool them, Todd," the hairdresser said while clipping the man's hair. She was wearing lots of dangly bracelets that clinked together as she worked. "Teachers are great, but let's face it, they're just doing a job. Now a mother, on the other hand—her kid is the center of her universe, so of course she's going to be more invested in—"

The hairdresser paused midsentence as she noticed Yasmin.

"Hello, dear," she said, lowering her scissors. "You're not . . . How did you find this place?"

The lie came easily enough. "My mom's friend recommended you. She gets her hair cut here all the time."

"Gotcha. What's your mom's friend's name?"

"Jennifer, I think."

The woman smiled. "Oh, Jenn. Sure. My name is Ms. Goffel. But you probably knew that already, your mom being such a regular and all."

"Not my mom. My mom's friend."

"Right."

Ms. Goffel looked more like a cool grandma than a witch, but Yasmin knew from firsthand experience how deceiving appearances could be. *Be careful*, she thought. *This one isn't a fake witch like Natacha. She's the real deal.*

Ms. Goffel returned to cutting the man's hair. Her scissor work was fast and efficient. "What's your name, sweetheart?" she asked. *Clip-clip, clip-clip.*

"Layla," Yasmin said, just in case Natacha had mentioned her real name at some point.

"Have a seat. I'll be with you in a moment."

Yasmin was too nervous to sit, however. She was thinking about the storefront window that was invisible from the street, and the fact that the hair salon was way too big to squeeze between the pizzeria and dry cleaner. This was a magic place, no doubt about it—just like Natacha's apartment. The similarity made her heart race.

Get out of here. Now.

"Oh, man," Yasmin said, pretending to check her phone. "I just remembered. I have to call my mom about something. I'll be right back."

"Aww. Such a good daughter."

Yasmin turned to leave. The back door had vanished.

No, Yasmin thought, running her hands over the brick wall. *I'm such an idiot. Why did I come here?*

"Have a seat," Ms. Goffel said. The smile had vanished from her face. "I'm almost done with Mr. Randolph here. After that you and I can have a little chat."

In a daze, Yasmin wandered over to the tiny waiting area and sat down. A small TV angled in her direction was playing a talk show with the volume off. From here, Yasmin was able to look directly into the long mirror opposite the barber's chair. There was nothing unusual about Ms. Goffel's reflection. Mr. Randolph was a different story. Although the man in the barber's seat looked normal enough to the naked eye, his reflection was that of a decomposing corpse. Maggots fell from Ms. Goffel's scissors as she clipped his lank dead hair.

Yasmin screamed.

"Manners," Ms. Goffel said in a stern voice, removing the smock from Mr. Randolph with a dramatic flourish. "I think he looks quite dapper myself."

To the naked eye, at least, this was true. Mr. Randolph's perfectly coiffed hair gave him the look of a man asking the questions in a job interview. He rose from the chair with a vacant expression and exited through the front door. Yasmin did her best not to look in the mirror as he left.

Ms. Goffel patted the chair. "Your turn, Layla."

"I don't need a haircut."

"Your split ends disagree."

Yasmin heard an insistent thumping sound from the back of the salon. The door had returned, and the next customer was eager to enter.

"Hold your horses!" Ms. Goffel yelled. She spun the barber's chair in Yasmin's direction. "There needs to be a customer in this seat at all times. That's one of the terms of my imprisonment. So if you don't sit here"—*thump, thump, thump*—"I'm afraid my next customer may get a little worked up. And that would be bad for both of us, sweetie. If you'd rather leave"—she nodded toward the front door—"go right ahead. You might get a bit of a headache later, but other than that it's perfectly safe. I hope you stay, though. I don't get many visitors with a pulse."

Thump. Thump. Thump.

Yasmin ran to the front door and pulled it open, setting off a little bell hanging above the frame. She could hear the traffic and feel the warm breeze on her face. Ms. Goffel wasn't lying. She was free to leave. But what would that accomplish? Yasmin had come here looking for a way to help Alex. Was she really going to give up so easily?

Yasmin closed the door and hopped into the chair. The pounding on the door instantly stopped.

164

"I guess I could use a trim," said Yasmin.

"Not with these," Ms. Goffel said, raising the scissors she had used on Mr. Randolph so Yasmin could take a closer look. Their handles were carved from solid bone, and the light danced strangely off their glistening blades. "These are intended for a very specific clientele—the dead, as you've probably figured out by now. If I were to use them on you . . ." She playfully snipped the scissors within an inch of Yasmin's nose. "Let's just say it would be the last haircut you'd ever get."

Ms. Goffel set her bone shears on the counter and began riffling through a drawer.

"Are you really a witch?" Yasmin asked.

Ms. Goffel gave her a probing look. "You're unusually well informed. I used to be a witch. Now I do this. Not by choice, mind you. There was a girl in a tower with the longest, most beautiful hair, and I loved her like a daughter—"

Yasmin gasped. "Wait! Are you talking about Rapun—"

Ms. Goffel slammed her hand down on the counter.

"Do not speak that name!" she exclaimed. "It brings back bad memories. And don't get me started on that story. One-sided, much?" She took a deep breath to regain her composure. "Anyway, after the nameless one's wedding to her precious prince, I came to the castle with my tail between my legs, trying to set things right. I even admitted that I had, perhaps, gone just a tiny bit overboard with the whole tower thing. She didn't want to hear it. Something about 'stealing the best years of her life.' She used her newfound wealth to hire a powerful enchantress, and she imprisoned me in this infernal salon, doomed to cut the hair of the dead for all eternity. Some serious 'the punishment fits the crime' vibes, right? I've always wondered if my baby girl paid extra for that." Ms. Goffel pulled a pair of normal-looking scissors from the drawer and raised them triumphantly. "Aha! For the living!"

"You really can't leave?" Yasmin asked.

"Not even for coffee," Ms. Goffel said, dripping some clear oil on the blades of the scissors and spreading it with a rag. "It wouldn't be so bad if it wasn't for the boredom. No books. No plays. No music. Just snick, snick, snick— next customer, please!" She tied a fresh smock around Yasmin's neck and removed the scrunchie from her hair, allowing it to fall free. "So pretty. Shame to hide it in a ponytail. Want me to curl it for you?"

"No, thank you."

"Just a trim, then," Ms. Goffel said with a sigh of disappointment. She made the first cut. "Is your name really Layla?"

"No. It's Yasmin."

"Much better." Ms. Goffel nodded toward the back door. "That entrance only appears to those who are looking for it. The dead are drawn here like flies, but the living who know about this place are few and far between. So how did you find me?"

Yasmin carefully considered how much she should reveal. Ms. Goffel seemed nice enough, but she might not look kindly upon Yasmin's involvement in the death of two witches.

Tell her just enough so she can help. No more than that.

Once Yasmin started talking, however, her initial wariness mysteriously vanished, and the events of the previous year spilled from her mouth in an unstoppable deluge. She started from the time she'd first knocked on Natacha's door, explained how she and Alex had escaped, and ended with the revelation that Simeon was a special type of vampire called a nachpyr. By the time she had finished, Yasmin's throat was parched.

"Why did I tell you all that?" she asked in bewilderment. Then Yasmin remembered who she was talking to, and her shoulders slumped. "You cast a spell on me, didn't you?"

Ms. Goffel shook her head. "Just a little honesty oil. That's what I wiped on the shears earlier. One of Natacha's most effective concoctions, in my humble opinion. Of course, thanks to you, I'll never be able to replenish my stock when it's gone—or any of her other oils. I'm not so happy about that." Yasmin grew nervous for a moment before Ms. Goffel smiled. "On the other hand—good riddance! I always suspected she was stealing Griselda's magic. That little parasite got what she deserved." She pulled Yasmin's hair over her forehead. "How do you feel about bangs?"

"The same way I feel about witches."

"Ouch. A nachpyr, huh. I thought they were extinct. Terrifying creatures in their heyday. Maybe they didn't drink blood like their cousins, but they certainly left their mark in other ways. I knew this one farm girl who was visited by a nachpyr three nights in a row. Well, you can't just suck fear out of people without knocking a few pieces loose, and this poor girl spent the rest of her days just lying there and staring into space, apart from the occasional screaming. You ask me, that's even crueler than death. Anyway, the humans caught wind of what was happening and went nachpyr hunting. My guess is Simeon burrowed into the world of dreams to hide. He's safe there. Weak—but safe."

Yasmin still didn't trust Ms. Goffel, especially after her use of the honesty oil, but she sounded like she knew her stuff.

"I'm worried about my friend," Yasmin said. "It's only a matter of time before Simeon does something terrible to him."

"You're probably right."

"Can you help me?"

Ms. Goffel gently brushed Yasmin's hair. "No maggots. Such a nice change of pace. You seem like a good kid. Go home. Hug your mom. Forget this business altogether."

"But Alex . . ."

". . . is going to die," Ms. Goffel said. "We all do eventually. Tell you what. If he comes my way, I promise to give him a fantastic haircut. Feel better?"

"No! You're a witch—a famous one! You must be able to help me!"

"I can't even help myself. Go home, Yasmin, and don't come back here again. You smell like the outside world, and it's making me sad."

Ms. Goffel removed Yasmin's smock and ushered her out of the chair. As soon as Yasmin's feet touched the floor, the pounding on the back door recommenced. "Come in!" Ms. Goffel announced. A slender woman wearing a blue sundress entered the salon and sat in the barber's chair. Yasmin took a quick glance at the mirror and an even quicker glance away.

"Please," Yasmin said. "He's my best friend. I can't just forget about him."

"You came here because you wanted an expert, right? Well, here's my expert opinion. Your friend is beyond our reach. There's no way to save him, and if you try, you're only going to get yourself killed—or worse. Is that what Alex would want?"

Ms. Goffel turned away and started clipping the woman's hair.

"Now, what shall we do here, Mrs. Clarke?" she asked. "A stylish bob, perhaps? Do we risk a perm? You'll be looking at this hairstyle for all eternity, so think carefully before you decide. . . ."

14

A CUP OF TEA

After dinner, Alex spent a few hours rummaging through his old stories. Some of them were downright awful, but he still enjoyed rereading them (especially his old Frisbee Man comics). It was like going through family photos; the awkwardness was part of the fun. On a few occasions, Alex found an outline or unfinished story that matched an engraving in the dream graveyard. He read these snippets eagerly, searching for clues, but they were never as helpful as he hoped. Alex had grown as a writer, and his old ideas didn't fit him anymore. Still, he couldn't escape the feeling that there was something in those forgotten notebooks and yellowed scraps of paper that could help him. He just didn't know what.

Before going to sleep that night, he hugged his mom and dad, which was something he had started to do on a nightly basis—a change in routine that his parents regarded with both pleasure and concern. Alex hoped he would wake up in the morning, but he wanted to make sure his parents knew he loved them, just in case. He couldn't stop thinking about the surprised look on Natacha's face as Simeon's stinger struck her neck. She had never seen it coming.

Would the same thing happen to him?

Alex glanced over at his copy of *Something Wicked This Way Comes* on the bedside table. It had been a long time since he'd opened it—or any other book, for that matter. Alex was exhausted all the time, and his body always felt sore, like he had the flu. Although he was technically sleeping eight hours every night, there was nothing restorative about his time in the dream graveyard. In a way, it was more like antisleep. Instead of resting, his mind was working harder than ever, and his anxiety was through the roof. Alex could see the toll it was taking every time he looked in the mirror.

How long can I keep this up? he wondered.

Before getting into bed, Alex dug through his closet until he found his old stuffed turtle. It had been years since he'd slept with Igor, but it felt right tonight. Alex supposed he missed the days when his nightmares were make-believe.

He turned off the light.

Yasmin's safe, he thought, holding Igor close. *That's all that matters.*

That night's dream was particularly taxing. Alex had to visit four grave worlds before he finally came up with a decent idea, and then it took him forever to lure the rest of the story to the surface. He needed sleep—real sleep. He was too exhausted to think straight, let alone perform the mental gymnastics required to create an imaginary world and characters.

As Simeon read the words etched into the gravestone, Alex stood nervously to the side, hoping this new story would satisfy him.

DRY-ERASE BOARD

It was Neil's first day at his new school. Since he was starting in the middle of the year, all the regular lockers had already been taken, so he was assigned a rusty old relic that had been dragged out of storage. It looked like it hadn't been used in years. Neil hung pictures of his old friends inside the door, along with a small dry-erase board to help him stay organized. The door was dented outward in several places and didn't close correctly, so there was no way to engage the lock.

Neil just left it open. He didn't want to be late on his first day.

When he returned to his locker that afternoon to get his lunch, Neil was feeling lonelier than ever. No one had said a single word to him. By this point in the year, the students were already set in their friendships, and they had no interest in getting to know a new kid. Neil missed his old friends more than ever.

When he opened the locker door, there was a message waiting for him on the dry-erase board.

Hi! ☺

At first, Neil was mad that someone had opened his locker. After checking to make sure that his stuff was untouched, however, he decided it wasn't a big deal. *At least someone in this school is friendly,* he thought. He erased the message and wrote one of his own.

Hi! I'm Neil. Who is this?

When he opened his locker at the end of the day, a reply was waiting for him:

My name's Cooper. You're new, right? I hope you like it here!

Neil smiled. After being ignored by his classmates all day, it was nice to make a friend.

Over the next week, Neil exchanged dozens of messages with Cooper. It turned out that Neil and his mysterious new pen pal had a lot in common. They both loved to read. Neither of them had ever flown on a plane. And they agreed that the other kids at school could be really annoying.

Whenever Neil asked if the two of them could meet in person, the answer was always the same:

That's not a good idea.

Neil asked around to see if someone at school knew a boy named Cooper, thinking he might find him that way, but no one did. Eventually he gave up and settled for conversations that took days to finish and long games of hangman and tic-tac-toe. Neil wished things were different, but it would have to do for now. He figured Cooper would eventually grow bored of their current arrangement and agree to meet in person.

It was only a matter of time.

A few weeks passed. By then, Neil had finally made some new friends. He still exchanged messages with Cooper, but not as many as before. The game had grown old. Questions were left unanswered, hangman puzzles left unsolved.

Neil arrived early one morning for band practice and found this message waiting for him:

Why don't you want to be friends anymore?

Neil replied:

I DO want to be friends.
But only if we can hang out in person.

He started to walk away, curious what Cooper's response would be that afternoon. After a few steps, however, he heard a squeaky noise behind him. It was the sound a dry-erase marker makes when writing on a board.

Neil opened the locker and his mouth fell open. A new message had appeared:

If that's what you really want.

The back wall of the locker had vanished, revealing a dark void. The air was suddenly as cold as a winter's night. Neil's breath cast misty plumes.

He heard the squeaking of a marker again and watched as the message on the dry-erase board changed on its own.

come closer

Neil's legs turned to jelly. He collapsed to the floor, too scared to move. All he could do was stare into the impossible darkness. A child stepped out of it. He was the same age as Neil, with sad eyes and a mouth frozen in a perpetual scream. His fingernails were torn and bloody.

Squeaksqueaksqueak.

A new message appeared.

friends? forever?

Neil shook his head. Cooper looked down, hurt. When he looked up again, a terrifying change had come over his face. His eyes bulged from their sockets, red-veined with rage. He leaned forward, gripping the edge of the locker with one hand while reaching for Neil's ankle with the other. With shocking clarity, Neil realized that Cooper was trapped in that tiny space. If Neil could move out of range, he would be safe. A foot or two. That's all it would take.

Neil started to crab-walk backward.

He almost made it.

The old custodian was annoyed he had to lug the locker all the way back down to the basement again. He had warned the principal not to bring the cursed thing upstairs in the first place:

"There was this kid, Cooper Miles, that used to be a student here a long time ago," the custodian had said. "He got bullied a lot. One of the things they did in those days was stuff you in a locker. Well, this kid got locked inside on the last day of school, and no one heard him screaming and banging—you can still see the dents on the inside of the door—because they left him there over summer vacation. They only found him when the body began to smell."

The principal had rolled his eyes at that and nearly fired the custodian on the spot when he later suggested the locker might have something to do with Neil Burkart's disappearance. Now here he was, returning the locker to its original home like nothing had happened. The custodian wanted to get rid of it entirely, but the principal had said no. They were short on lockers—budget cuts—and who knew when another new student might arrive.

The custodian dragged the locker off the rolling cart and pushed it against the wall. As he was about to leave, he heard a squeaking sound behind the locker door. He opened it. They had removed all of the missing boy's things except a dry-erase board. On it was written:

HELP ME

The custodian crept forward for a closer look and saw a blue-veined hand with bloody fingernails wipe the words away before the locker door slammed shut.

This flower was the strangest one yet, a paper-thin white rectangle that looked more like a leaf than a petal. Delicate veins formed the word "Hi!"

Simeon carefully unearthed the treasure and took a deep whiff of its fragrance.

"Glorious," he whispered, and the veins of the flower shifted to form the word. "Such an imaginative bouquet, spiced with fear. I think this might be your finest tale, Alex. I have to confess, my sympathies lie with Cooper. I felt the same way as him when I was disguised in my jackal form, my longing for friendship making me afraid to show my true self."

"Is that what you think we are?" Alex asked. "Friends?"

Simeon stared at him for a long time. Alex felt like the nachpyr's eerie eyes were looking past his flesh and bone to the inner workings of his heart.

"Come with me," Simeon said.

As they walked across the graveyard, Alex studied the back of Simeon's neck, where a flap of reddish skin, similar to the one hanging from his left ear, billowed with every step. He wondered how it worked. Did Simeon need to move the flap himself, providing clearance for his stinger to emerge? Or was he able to simply call it forth at will?

Alex suspected he was about to find out.

Given such dire expectations, he was shocked by their destination: a skeletal tree that looked like a Halloween greeting card. Beneath its branches was a beautiful chestnut table bearing a cast-iron teapot, a single cup, and a wooden chess set. All the pieces were monsters. The white king was Dracula, while the black pieces were led by Frankenstein (and the Bride of Frankenstein as the queen, of course). The rest of the set was composed of various wolfmen, mummies, and ghosts, with zombies as the pawns.

Simeon took a seat and gestured for Alex to do the same.

"I thought you'd like this particular chess set," Simeon said with an almost-bashful look. "Do you play?"

"Um . . . yeah," managed Alex, still in a state of shock. "I'm not very good, though."

"That doesn't matter to me. I miss the game itself."

Simeon moved a white zombie two spaces forward and began picking the flower apart. Alex watched, speechless, as the nachpyr lifted the lid of the teapot—releasing a cloud of steam—and dumped the pieces into the water.

"I can't wait to see what this one taste likes," he said.

Alex stared at the teapot in disbelief. He had come up with a dozen theories that might explain the purpose of the flowers. Tea had not made the list.

"That's why you've been keeping me a prisoner here?" Alex snapped, his face flushed with anger. "So you can enjoy a nice cup of *tea*?"

A wan smile curled Simeon's lips.

"It's a little more complicated than that. I'll tell you all about it after you make your move."

Alex quickly opened with his knight, as he always did—or, in this case, his Creature from the Black Lagoon.

"I was human once," Simeon said as he studied the board. "A fearful wisp of a boy who jumped at every shadow and suffered from horrible nightmares. One night I was visited by a vampire. He said my fear was so pungent he could smell it from two villages away. Would I like to become one of them? Or would I like to die?" Simeon shrugged. "It was an easy choice."

He poured himself a cup of tea and swirled it around. It had a faint medicinal smell. Simeon took a sip and smiled.

"Natacha was right. You're exactly what I needed."

"That didn't stop you from killing her."

"I thought you would be pleased about that. She was your enemy."

"Nothing about this pleases me."

Simeon moved another zombie, clearing the path for his wolfman. Alex immediately countered with a zombie of his own.

"I don't like to think about those early days as a regular vampire," Simeon said. "The bloodlust. The hunger. It was all so . . . unrefined. Finally, as I mentioned, there were those of us who broke away from the pack and became nachpyrs. That was when my true life began. Consuming fear isn't a mindless act, like plunging your fangs into a victim's neck. There's an art to it, a craft. While your host is sleeping, you slip into their dreams and shape their nightmares. You want them as terrified as possible. The more powerful the fear, the more fortifying the meal. I was an extraordinary weaver of nightmares, Alex. You would have been impressed."

They exchanged zombies. Alex noticed that his Frankenstein was exposed and moved his mummy to protect him.

"Alas, humans finally caught on and began hunting us, and I fled into the realm of dreams. They sent their witches and shamans to find me, but they were woefully overmatched. Even the simplest dream is an infinity of infinities, and I had an endless number of them at my fingertips. I figured I would hide until the nachpyrs were forgotten, and I could once again hunt in peace. I stayed a lot longer than I planned."

"Because you were scared," Alex said. He saw a flash of anger in Simeon's eyes and knew he had hit the mark. The nachpyr poured a second cup of tea and blew on it thoughtfully.

"At last, I risked a reappearance," Simeon continued. "The moment I regained my physical form, starvation struck me, and I quickly found a suitable victim. When I tried to create a nightmare, however, I couldn't do it.

Imagination is like a muscle, Alex. Without use, it withers and dies. For centuries, I'd been little more than a watcher of other people's dreams, and this passive existence had stripped me of my creativity. In short, I had no way to feed. I barely made it back to the dream realm alive."

Alex could see that Simeon was planning to trap his Frankenstein through a combination of his Phantom of the Opera, Dracula's Bride, and a pesky zombie that refused to die. Alex could sacrifice his own Bride to facilitate his king's escape, but that would only prolong the inevitable. He decided to capture Simeon's wolfman instead. It was a meaningless move, but Alex didn't want to go down without a fight.

"The years passed," Simeon said. "While I brooded and nursed my wounds, I sensed some truly astounding nightmares, unlike anything I'd felt in a long, long time. My curiosity was aroused. I had to know who it was."

"My nightmares are really that bad? I hardly ever remember them."

"Not you. Yasmin."

Alex looked up from the board in surprise.

"It's impossible for me to feed here," Simeon said. "All I can do is . . . exist. But Yasmin's dreams were so vivid, so horrifying, that I could practically taste them." Simeon rubbed his misshapen ear. "She had escaped Natacha's apartment physically, but in all the important ways she was still there. It's a wonder her mind didn't crack entirely. I decided to find the splendid witch who had caused such torment. Fortunately, although Natacha's physical body was long gone, her spirit was still clinging to this world like an angry ghost, refusing to leave. She reminded me of myself as a child—afraid of death and willing to pay any price to avoid it. She told me all about you, Alex, and after that I started visiting your dreams. Eventually I found this miraculous graveyard. I had seen such places before. Libraries of memories, a filing cabinet of wishes, alphabetized fears. Even in dreams, the human mind seeks to make order out of chaos." Simeon grinned, looking for just a moment like a true child. "Never seen a story graveyard, though. That's a new one."

Alex couldn't help feeling a little pleased. He liked being original.

"I knew we were kindred spirits from the start, Alex. Both of us understand that fear is something to be treasured, not locked away. I should have shown you my true face from the start. But you had already written such marvelous stories under Natacha's care, so I figured it was best to let her take the lead. Besides, it's always safer to be the one lurking in the shadows."

"You're a coward."

"I'm a survivor." Simeon slid his mummy across the board. "Checkmate. Another game?"

Alex could hear the loneliness in Simeon's voice and felt an instinctive jolt of sympathy. He reminded himself that this wasn't a ten-year-old boy. It was an ancient creature without remorse.

"I only play chess with my friends," Alex said.

Simeon looked hurt. "Why can't we be friends? You certainly have more in common with me than Yasmin. I'm a creator, just like you."

"Then write your own stories."

Alex's words clearly hit a nerve. Simeon rose from his seat, knocking over his cup and spilling tea across the table. "You think I *like* doing this?" he snapped. "It's humiliating, drinking your pathetic dregs in the hope of returning to some semblance of my former self! But what choice do I have?" He took a moment to regain his composure and began returning the chess pieces to their starting positions. "After I found your graveyard, I made a few adjustments that allowed me to distill your stories into a tonic for my lost imagination. That's what the tea is for. A kind of . . . creative rehabilitation."

"You're stealing my imagination?" Alex asked in disgust.

"Of course not," Simeon said, looking offended at the suggestion. "Each flower captures the creative energy you used to write that particular story—no more, no less. Think of it like recycling. You empty some creativity into a story, and I reuse it to restore my own imagination. It's working, too. I'm already feeling a little stronger. In just a few years or so, I'll be able to create my own nightmares again. After that I can return to the real world—and feed."

"What happens to the people you feed on?" Alex asked. "Is it like with a vampire . . . ?"

"You mean do they die?" Simeon asked.

"Yes."

"Are you concerned, or are you curious?"

"A little of both," Alex confessed.

"One visit doesn't cause any permanent effects."

Alex sighed with relief.

"But no self-respecting nachpyr would ever stop with one visit," Simeon continued. "It takes a few tries to understand a dreamer's fears and create the perfect nightmare. Unfortunately, once they've reached that level of all-consuming fear, their weak human hearts do tend to give out."

Alex felt sick to his stomach. If Simeon returned to the waking world with his old abilities intact, people were going to die—and it would be Alex's fault.

"I'd like to leave now," he said. "I haven't been feeling so great lately."

Simeon didn't look surprised. "I was wondering when that would become an issue. Humans aren't meant to spend so much time in the dream world. They're a fragile species."

"Let me go, then. Easy fix."

"It's nice to see you haven't lost your sense of humor. That's one of the reasons I like you, Alex. Don't worry, though. I've already thought of an even better solution. Until tomorrow, then. And please consider what I said about us being friends. I could help you with your chess game! No offense, but you need it."

"I'll write your stories, but you and I will never be friends."

Simeon scratched the back of his neck.

"We'll see about that," he said.

15

NOT A WITCH

Yasmin returned to Snip, Snap, Snout the next day and brought Ms. Goffel a cup of coffee from the deli down the block.

"You're wasting your time," Ms. Goffel said.

Yasmin put the coffee on the counter and took a seat. Ms. Goffel did her best to ignore the cup as she went about her business, but finally the temptation grew too great. She removed the lid and inhaled its 99-cent aroma as though it were the finest wine, then took a lingering sip. Yasmin thought she saw the witch wipe a tear from her eye.

"This doesn't change a thing," Ms. Goffel said. "I still can't help you."

The witch refused to speak to her again, though she did casually mention to a young man getting a buzz cut that she had always enjoyed her coffee with one sugar and a splash of cream.

The next day, Yasmin brought her exactly that. Ms. Goffel still ignored her, but she did tell two different customers all about her lifelong love for crullers.

Yasmin made an extra stop at the bakery before arriving the next day.

This turned into Yasmin's regular routine. After school, she would take the train straight to Queensboro Plaza, place her bribe on the counter, and wait for Ms. Goffel to acknowledge her presence. After exactly an hour, Yasmin would give up for the day and go next door to grab a quick slice. Their pizza was growing on her.

Eventually, Yasmin started to bring Lenore, who had been spending more and more time at her house. Though she refused to admit it, Ms. Goffel enjoyed the cat's presence, sporadically putting down the bone shears to give the cat an affectionate scratch between the ears. During one visit, she gently touched Lenore's ruined tail, which looked worse than ever.

"The nachpyr did this?" Ms. Goffel asked. Her eyes had grown dark and scary. Yasmin thought she was glimpsing a little of the old witch, back when the mere mention of her name made babies cry and villagers lock their doors.

"He's a monster," Yasmin said, stroking Lenore. "Help me stop him."

Ms. Goffel looked thoughtful for a moment, then shook her head. "I have to get back to work."

The routine continued. Coffee, cruller, cat—and no conversation at all.

Yasmin began to wonder if Ms. Goffel was right. Maybe she *was* wasting her time. She wished Alex was there. Grown-ups loved him. He would have had Ms. Goffel eating out of the palm of his hand by now.

Besides, she missed him.

A quick text can't hurt, Yasmin thought, longing to contact her friend. *Just a sentence or two to let him know I haven't abandoned him. Surely Simeon would never know. . . .*

Except he might. Yasmin was still afraid he was watching her, unseen. For the past few weeks, she had felt a kind of creeping dread whenever she left her house, as though someone was constantly on her tail. Maybe she was just being paranoid. Maybe not. Either way, she couldn't risk contacting Alex. She wished Lenore could at least tell him about their trips to the hair salon, but that was a bad idea as well. Simeon was inside Alex's mind. What if he could read it?

Yasmin was so worried about him.

Ms. Goffel has to help. I won't give up until she does.

School ended. The days grew hot and sticky. Yasmin continued to visit Snip, Snap, Snout. At last, there was a break in the routine. After straightening the unruly hair of a teenage girl wearing overalls, Ms. Goffel patted the barber's chair and turned in Yasmin's direction.

"Those split ends are driving me nuts," she said.

Yasmin hopped into the chair before the witch could change her mind. Ms. Goffel gave her a smock and switched out the bone shears for a normal pair of scissors.

"Have you changed your mind about bangs?" she asked.

"That's a big no."

"Too bad. I enjoyed the coffee. The crullers were a little dry. No one knows how to make a good cruller anymore. But still—thank you."

"You're welcome."

"I've thought about your problem. I'd like to help you— truly, I would—but my hands are tied. There's a reason that sneaky nachpyr is hiding in other people's dreams. Not even magic can touch him there."

"Why don't we just pull him into the real world, then?"

Ms. Goffel laughed. "Oh, how I love youthful optimism! Do you know a spell that can accomplish that, Yasmin? Because I sure don't. And, just between me and you—I know a lot of spells."

"But . . . theoretically . . . if we could get Simeon into the real world . . ."

"There might be something we could try. *Might.* But don't get your hopes up—unless you can figure out a way to get him here, of course."

Yasmin thought about it while Ms. Goffel trimmed her hair. Finally, she came up with an idea. It was flawed, to say the least, but it was better than nothing.

"When Alex finishes a story," Yasmin said, "the grave world destroys itself. What if Simeon was trapped inside when that happened?"

"Didn't you already try that with Natacha? I doubt Simeon's thick enough to fall for the same trick."

"Assume he did. Would that be enough to get rid of him?"

"I believe so. He would die, I think, or at the very least spend eternity floating through the dream ether, which amounts to the same thing. But it won't work. Nachpyrs are notoriously powerful dream walkers. The moment Simeon is threatened, he'll just hop into someone else's dream. It would be as easy as me or you walking through a door—well, you, at least." Ms. Goffel's scissors suddenly froze midclip. "Unless, of course, he was bound to the dream by magic. That would be a different story entirely."

"I thought you said magic didn't work in dreams."

"No. I said it was impossible to pull a nachpyr into the real world against his will. Such a spell doesn't exist. But temporarily binding a nachpyr to a dream? That's possible." Ms. Goffel began rummaging through the drawer beneath the mirror. "It won't be easy. Your friend will have to lure Simeon into a grave world, bind him to it, and then destroy it. If he can pull that off—we can make it so Simeon can't escape to another dream. He'll have no choice but to return to the waking world."

Ms. Goffel dug out an envelope that read "Baby's First Haircut" and removed a long strand of golden-blond hair. It glowed with a heavenly radiance.

"Whoa," Yasmin said in awe. "Is that Rapun—her hair?"

"My last strand. It possesses extraordinary magic, even in dreams. Grows like wildfire and can't be broken. Your friend can use this to incapacitate the nachpyr. It won't imprison him forever, but it'll force him to abandon ship if the world is collapsing around him."

She explained what Alex needed to do and found a special pouch that would allow him to transport the hair into his dream.

"Thank you," Yasmin said, taking the objects. "This is your last strand, though. Are you sure?"

"I think it's time I let go of the past. In any case, I'm not giving you this for free, young lady. There's something I want in return."

"Anything," Yasmin said, wondering if the plan was doomed to fail before it even started. The price for such a precious treasure had to be steep, and she was worried about her ability to pay it.

"If you somehow manage to rescue the storyteller," Ms.

Goffel said, "could he come here and read me one of his stories? After everything you've told me, I'm rather curious. Besides, that TV over there only gets the one channel, and the volume doesn't even work. I'm desperate for entertainment."

Yasmin sighed with relief. "You help me save Alex, and I promise he'll read you as many stories as you want!"

They shook on it.

"Okay, then," Ms. Goffel said. "Let's assume Alex does his job and forces the nachpyr into the real world. Once he's here, getting back isn't nearly as easy—and he'll be weak, too. We should be able to use magic to destroy him completely. Unfortunately, I can't leave this salon, so unless you can convince Simeon that he really needs a haircut, you're going to have to cast the spell yourself."

"Umm . . . small problem. I'm not a witch."

"Doesn't matter. The power of any spell comes from the energy of the caster. A true witch is able to channel her own energy without assistance. A nonwitch like yourself, however, can rely on totems instead."

"Right. Totems. Big fan. I assume you've got a few of those in the big drawer of magical objects over there?"

Ms. Goffel rubbed her forehead like a teacher who realizes her class is woefully unprepared for a lesson.

"That's not how it works. Totems aren't a one-size-fits-all kind of deal, like a wand or enchanted ring. They change from spell to spell. It's all about creating a link between the caster and the target. Since a nachpyr's entire existence revolves around fear, I think your totems should as well."

"Meaning what, exactly?"

"You'll need three objects that symbolize your deepest, darkest fears. Those totems, along with a short incantation, will allow you to channel enough energy to entrap and destroy Simeon."

Ms. Goffel's next customer banged on the door, growing impatient.

"I'm sorry, but you have to go," Ms. Goffel said, removing Yasmin's smock. "I'm already behind, and when the queue gets too long . . . well, let's just say people in the neighborhood start to disappear."

"Three objects that I'm scared of," Yasmin said, running it over in her head. "Easy. I hate worms, so I can dig up a few of those. And maybe a clown's nose would—"

"Those are just childish fears," Ms. Goffel said, shaking her head. "They're not nearly powerful enough to be used as totems. Think about it this way. There are two doors. The first one leads to instant death. You'll live if you take the second door, but there's something behind it that fills you with such bone-quivering, blinding terror that you think, 'Maybe I should take the first door after all.' That's the level of fear you need, Yasmin. So tell me.

What's behind door number two?"

Yasmin's entire body grew numb. There was only one answer.

"Natacha's apartment."

Ms. Goffel smiled. "Good. If you want to save your friend, that's where you need to go."

16

AN UNWANTED GIFT

"Checkmate," said Simeon, taking a sip of tea.

Alex stared at the pieces with a slack-jawed expression. It was hard for him to remember what they did anymore. Just moving them from square to square required a titanic effort.

He was so tired.

"Another game?" Simeon asked.

Alex looked up at the painted moon. It was nearly time for the rain to fall and the sun to take its place in the sky. From what Alex could tell, that meant his body had once again missed its opportunity to enjoy a normal night of sleep. Try as he might, he couldn't make up for this lost time; his confused body refused to take naps or sleep late. It was like being caught in a permanent jet lag.

"Please let me sleep," Alex said.

Simeon crossed his arms and pouted. "We barely had time to play—if you can even call that *playing*. It took you forever to finish your story tonight. You need to work faster."

"I *can't*. I need a break. One night of real sleep, I'm begging you. I'll be better after that."

Simeon scoffed. "You want a night off? You need to *earn* it. That tea tonight was weak. You're slipping up."

"I'm trying. I'm just so *tired*."

Simeon's sour expression turned sympathetic. It was like this with him. One moment he was the soulless nachpyr, willing to drain Alex of his creativity until he was nothing but a withered husk. The next moment he was a little boy who seemed genuinely moved by Alex's plight. Initially, Simeon's fickle nature had offered Alex the hope that the nachpyr might one day set him free. Now he just found it annoying. At least with Natacha, he had always known where he stood.

"Would you like to brainstorm some story ideas?" Simeon asked eagerly. "I feel a little of my old imagination starting to return. I'm sure I'll be a lot more useful than that girl, at least."

"I don't need help. I need sleep."

"That reminds me, I've kept an eye on Yasmin, just like I

promised. She is doing *great*. I'm actually a little impressed how she's been able to put this whole experience in her rearview mirror. She even has a new best friend—sporty kid, very different than you. They're together all the time. He has such a knack for making her laugh. I wanted to let you know, in case you were worried about her. Don't be. She's fine."

Alex didn't respond. He wanted to be happy for Yasmin—he really did—but he couldn't help feeling a little resentful. Had she seriously forgotten about him already? He supposed he shouldn't be surprised. This wasn't the first time she had cut him loose.

You're the one who made the deal with Simeon, Alex reminded himself. *You can't get mad about it now.*

"I'm glad to hear she's doing well," he said, and mostly meant it.

Simeon seemed surprised by this response. "You're *glad*? You should be furious! You sacrificed yourself for this girl, and she forgot about you like that." He snapped his fingers.

"What else was she supposed to do? You made us promise not to talk to each other. She's just doing what you said."

"I don't understand your continued loyalty to that child. She moved on, Alex. You need to do the same. I can be a much better friend than she ever was. In fact"—he rose to his feet—"I'm prepared to give you the greatest gift you've ever received."

Simeon walked across the table, knocking chess pieces to the ground, and crouched in front of Alex like a wolf rearing for an attack.

"Every fear has a unique fragrance," he said. "The fear of dying smells like rotting flesh. The fear of being alone? Mothballs. Clowns? Popcorn. Heights? Burnt garlic." He saw Alex's perplexed expression and shrugged. "I've never understood that one either. But your fear is depressingly common." He leaned forward and sniffed Alex's hair. "The fear of failure. You think you'll never be as good as the authors you admire. And you're right. In this lifetime, at least. But given time, precious time . . . miraculous things can happen."

Alex broke out in a cold sweat. He was starting to see where Simeon was going with this.

"It's tempting to view storytelling as a kind of magic," the nachpyr said, "but you and I know the truth, don't we? It's a craft, plain and simple, no different than carpentry or shipbuilding. And how do you get better at a craft, Alex? You practice it. Some writers are geniuses. They're freaks of nature who are born great. But an average, moderately talented writer like yourself—all you need is *time*."

Alex heard a juicy sound, like fingers tearing apart the flesh of a grapefruit, and saw Simeon's spine stinger rise above his head. It hooked in Alex's direction, ready to strike.

"I'm going to make you a nachpyr, Alex. Think of all you can accomplish with an eternity to master your craft. You'll become the greatest writer who ever lived. That's my gift to you." He pointed at a tarry black substance dangling from the tip of the stinger. "See that ichor there? A little of my old fear, from when I was a child. I'm sure you know your vampire lore, Alex. In many traditions, a victim must drink the blood of a vampire to become a vampire. This is much the same." Simeon laughed. "But don't worry! You don't have to drink it! I'll just inject it directly into your veins."

"Don't," Alex whispered. He wanted to run, but the spine stinger seemed like a living, breathing thing, and he was afraid that any sudden movement might invite it to strike.

"You won't be tired anymore. Think of how nice that'll be. And all this human concern about 'right' and 'wrong'? Poof! Gone! All you'll know is hunger and how to satisfy it."

Simeon bent closer. Alex clenched the arms of his chair as the sharp tip of the stinger grazed his skin.

"You've always loved monsters," Simeon whispered. "Now you'll get to be one."

"No," Alex said. And then, with an intuition for

character born and bred through hundreds of stories, he added, "I thought you were my friend."

It was the right thing to say. Simeon's face fell.

"You've completely ruined the moment, Alex," he said, withdrawing his stinger. "This is supposed to be a cause for celebration. I'm giving you the greatest gift you'll ever receive. Is it so unreasonable to expect a little gratitude?" He plopped back into his seat with the look of a spoiled child who hadn't gotten the present he wanted. "I'll give you some time to think about how you've made me feel. Hopefully you'll have a better attitude tomorrow when I turn you—no excuses this time. And if you're still feeling ungrateful . . . that's okay. You'll thank me after you taste fear for the first time and realize what you've been missing. Awake."

Alex opened his eyes and saw Igor looking back at him. He sighed with relief and hugged the stuffed turtle tight.

"I'm still me," he whispered. "For now, at least."

Alex stumbled into the bathroom and checked his neck for puncture wounds. All clear. He continued to stare into the mirror, wondering if he'd be able to see his reflection when he woke up tomorrow. Were nachpyrs like vampires in this regard, or were they different? He hoped he never had the chance to find out. Simeon's words echoed in his head: *All you'll know is hunger and how to satisfy it.* In that way, it seemed, nachpyrs were exactly like their cousins. Being turned wouldn't just change Alex's feeding habits. He would become a soulless monster.

He'd hurt people.

Alex collapsed onto his bed and stared up at the ceiling. Did he have any options at all? What about running away? He had some money saved up, certainly enough for a bus ticket. If he kept downing energy drinks, maybe he could stay awake long enough to get as far from his family and friends as possible.

But what about the other people he hurt? And what if he came back here later? Fleeing would only delay the inevitable.

Lenore hopped onto his bed. Her stubby tail had hardened like a shell. It gave off a foul odor.

"Hey, buddy," Alex said. "We're quite the pair, aren't we?"

She was breathing heavily, and her paws were caked with mud. Lenore had been wandering off for hours on end lately and refused to let him know where she'd been. This time, however, she had returned with a leather pouch tied to her back. Inside were two objects. The first was a single strand of hair that glowed so brightly Alex had to shade his eyes to look at it. The second was a carefully folded letter written in handwriting he knew as well as his own. His heart leaped.

A—

I know we're not supposed to talk, but I have to take a chance here. Lenore and I have been busy, and there are some things you gotta know. . . .

Alex read the letter in astonishment and wonder—*she found another fairy-tale witch?*—then a second time, slowly, considering its implications. Simeon had lied. Yasmin hadn't forgotten about him at all; in fact, she had been working on a plan to save him this entire time! That alone was enough to rejuvenate his flagging spirits, but there was more. His friend—his *best* friend—had figured out a way they could defeat Simeon. Each of them had a role to play. Yasmin was vague about her part, on the off chance that Simeon could read Alex's mind. She was more straightforward about his assignment.

He needed to trap Simeon in a grave world.

"How?" Alex asked, running both hands through his hair.

Simeon was no fool. After what they'd pulled with Natacha, he'd kept his distance from all open graves, giving Alex zero opportunity to push him. Trying to drag him by brute force wasn't going to work either. Alex had a size advantage, but Simeon had a stinger.

What if I pretended to be his friend and tried to coax

him into one of the worlds?

This was a slightly better option, but it still seemed like a long shot. Simeon planned to change Alex into a nachpyr the next time they met. He would be on high alert for any kind of trick.

There must be an answer, Alex thought. *I'm just not seeing it yet.*

He considered the problem all day long. His brain was as fuzzy as a tennis ball, however, and all he could think of were the same tired plans that he had already dismissed. He felt like he was trapped in an endless loop, unable to escape. . . .

A new idea struck him like a thunderbolt.

Alex ran down to the basement. For weeks now, he had been combing through his old stories, unsure what he was looking for but sensing that there was an important answer waiting to be found. Now that Alex had a concrete objective, he dug through the boxes of scribbled notes and half-finished drafts with renewed fervor.

"Where are you?" he asked, tossing papers left and right. Alex couldn't let his entire plan ride on a guess. He needed proof. It had to be here! He searched every box, then started from the beginning and searched them a second time.

The story he was looking for didn't exist.

I was so sure, he thought, staring at the useless pages

now blanketing the basement floor.

"Holy cow," his mom said from the top of the basement steps. "Who set off the tornado?"

"Sorry, Mom," Alex said. "I'll clean it up."

"Don't worry about it. Just go to bed. You haven't been yourself lately."

You think I'm not myself now? Alex thought, dropping a mound of loose pages into the nearest box. *Just wait until tomorrow.*

"What are you even looking for?" Mrs. Mosher asked, coming downstairs.

"One of my old stories. I thought it could help me with something. But you know I save everything, so if it's not here, I never wrote it. I think it was just wishful thinking on my part."

Alex was about to dump another pile of papers into a box when his mother snatched them out of his hands. "You're going to mess them up," she said, stacking them into a neat pile. "Have you checked the purple bin?"

Alex gave his mom a blank look. "What purple bin?"

Mrs. Mosher crossed to a shelving unit packed with his brother's trophies. She shoved a few to the side and pulled out a large storage bin.

"Here you go," Mrs. Mosher said, placing it next to Alex. "These are your earliest stories, before you started saving them on your own." She ruffled his hair. "We always knew you were special. Weird, but special."

Alex stared at the bin in disbelief. He had never known.

"Don't stay up too late," Mrs. Mosher said. "You look like a ghost." She started up the stairs, then looked back over her shoulder. "Oh—your dad and I finally read that story you gave us. Sorry it took so long."

"What did you think?"

"I think everything you write is brilliant. You're my son. But you know I'm not a fan of the scary stuff."

"I know."

"That doesn't mean it wasn't a good story. It just wasn't for me. But you wait, Alex. There's a whole world out there that's going to love your books when you grow up. Your father and I are so proud of you. I know we don't tell you that enough, but we are."

Alex looked up at her with tears in his eyes. "Thanks, Mom."

He took a long breath and removed the lid of the bin. Maybe, just maybe, they might still have a chance.

17

THE RETURN

Yasmin stepped inside the elevator and pressed the button for the fourth floor. The car rose with a lurch. She leaned against the wall for support and tried to ignore the churning of her stomach. The elevator had been renovated since the last time she was here, and Yasmin didn't want to puke on the nice new floor.

The doors opened. She stepped into the hallway. The floor seemed to rock beneath her feet like a ship on a raging sea.

"Stay calm," Yasmin said. "Natacha doesn't live here anymore. It's just a building. Wood. Glass. Concrete."

The elevator doors closed behind her. Suddenly the short walk to the end of the hall seemed an incalculable distance. It wasn't too late to change her mind. The elevator car hadn't even left yet. Except how could she live with herself if she did that? Just a few hours earlier, Lenore had delivered a short reply from Alex, letting Yasmin know what would happen to him if she didn't gather the totems tonight.

Simply put: he wouldn't be Alex anymore.

Yasmin started down the hallway. The renovations here were even more extensive than the ones in the elevator: freshly painted walls, brand-new light fixtures, framed landscapes on the walls. It was almost enough to make Yasmin believe that the forces of darkness once inhabiting this place had truly moved on.

Almost.

She reached the end of the hall and stood before Natacha's old apartment. The metallic "4E" had been replaced by quaint ceramic tiles. Other than that, the door looked the same. She knocked on it. Inside, Yasmin could hear approaching footsteps. A young woman with close-cropped hair opened the door a few inches and peeked out, keeping the chain latched. She was wearing a tank top that showed off plenty of colorful tattoos.

"Hey there," the woman said.

"Hey," Yasmin replied. She took a deep breath; there was no going back after this. "This is really hard to explain, but . . . you know the story about what happened here, right?"

"'The Miraculous 58'? That whole thing?"

Yasmin nodded. After Aunt Gris died, the children who had been turned into porcelain figurines returned to life—at the exact same age as when they had been captured. None of them remembered what happened. The story was all over the internet for a solid two weeks until some famous couple broke up and everyone forgot about it.

"So . . . I know this may sound hard to believe," Yasmin continued, "but I . . ."

"You're one of the kids who walked out of this place."

"Um . . . yeah. And . . ."

"You'd like to come in and see if you remember anything. Or, at the very least, put the past behind you."

Yasmin took a closer look at the woman. "Are you some kind of psychic?" she asked.

The woman unlatched the door and smiled.

"You're not the first one of those kids to come here. Take as much time as you need. I'm Cheryl."

"Yasmin."

"Pretty name. Come on in."

Yasmin followed Cheryl into the apartment. It was hard to believe it was the same place. The creepy wallpaper and antique furnishings had been replaced by clean white walls and a cozy couch a few years past its prime. There was a TV in the corner, photographs on the shelves, and a half-eaten bag of potato chips on the coffee table.

The only thing remotely strange about the apartment

was how ordinary it looked.

"Nice place," Yasmin said.

"Thanks," said Cheryl. "I couldn't normally afford an apartment like this, but a lot of people were scared off by the whole Miraculous 58 thing, so the landlord had to lower the rent just to get a taker. Personally, I don't get it. What happened was weird, no doubt about that, but in the end a bunch of lost kids returned to their families. Sounds like happy-ending territory to me."

"That's one way of thinking about it," Yasmin said.

They went into the kitchen. Yasmin had spent countless hours here cooking meals for Natacha. It looked very different now. The curtains had been removed, permitting a constant supply of natural sunlight, and potted herbs filled the room with pleasing scents.

"You want some tea?" Cheryl asked as she began to unpack a few tote bags sitting on the counter. "I just went shopping. There was this big sale, so I snagged a few random ones, just to test them out." She examined a box and grimaced. "'Tomato mint' sounded better in the store."

"Thanks," Yasmin said. "I'd love some." Now that she was inside the apartment, she wasn't sure what to do next. A cup of tea might buy her some time to think. "So how many kids have come here?"

"I've lost count, honestly," Cheryl said as she unpacked her groceries. "Usually they show up in groups. Freaky

experience like that—must be easier when you have someone to share it with. You friends with any of them?"

"Just one," Yasmin said.

"That's good. At least you have someone you can talk
to. My friends think it's weird, just letting a bunch of kids
in my apartment whenever they show up, but I feel like
that's part of living here. I knew the history when I signed
the lease. Besides, I feel bad. It must be frustrating not
knowing what happened. Do you remember anything at
all?"

Yasmin shook her head. She didn't like lying to her
host, but she knew how crazy the truth would sound.

"What did the other kids do while they were here?"
Yasmin asked.

Cheryl filled a teakettle with water and put it on the
stove. "Just hung out. Some of them were hoping to jog
their memory, but most of the kids just wanted to prove
to themselves that they could step over the threshold. Ever
have nightmares about this place?"

Yasmin nodded.

"Them too. I think coming here was their way of putting fear in its place. I mean, sure, they could have easily
avoided this building for the rest of their lives. But who
wins then? We always talk about conquering fear, not
avoiding it. There's a reason for that." She raised two tea
bags. "Normal tea? Or are we feeling adventurous?"

"Whichever one you're having."

"Oh!" Cheryl said, remembering something. "The last woman who lived here—the one who disappeared—left these weird little items hidden around the house. I threw them all in a box, hoping there might be something there that could help you kids remember. It hasn't worked yet, but you're welcome to give it a shot if you're interested."

"That would be amazing," Yasmin said, not believing her luck.

Cheryl returned a few minutes later with a white box that had originally held reams of copy paper. She placed it on the kitchen table and served Yasmin her tea.

"Let me know if that's undrinkable. I'll be in the living room if you need anything."

Yasmin removed the lid of the box. It was packed with Natacha's belongings, mostly jewelry and makeup. Would any of them make a suitable totem? She was considering a pair of earrings when she spotted Natacha's old hairbrush, still covered with hair. *Bingo*, thought Yasmin. She knew from her oil-making days that hair and fingernails made excellent spell ingredients.

One down, two to go.

Yasmin kept digging and found the original "4E" that had once hung on the front door—another excellent totem. How many times had she seen that ominous letter-number combo in her nightmares, often with a fiery glow? She set it aside, grimacing at the feel of it against her bare skin, and continued her search.

As Yasmin neared the bottom of the box, she started to get nervous. What if she couldn't find a third totem? There was always the pair of earrings she had been considering earlier, but she still wasn't sold on them. The hairbrush and "4E" felt *right.* The earrings, not so much.

Finally, at the very bottom of the box, she found it.

Natacha's ledger.

Yasmin flipped through the pages, gazing in wonder at the familiar columns of names and purchases. Her neat handwriting filled the last few pages, solidifying the personal connection that would make the book an effective totem.

Hairbrush. 4E. Ledger.

Mission accomplished.

Yasmin took a celebratory sip of tea and winced; tomato mint tasted about as good as it sounded. She began to repack the box and noticed a glass vial beneath a bottom flap. It was filled with dark amber liquid that a white label identified as YOUTH OIL. Yasmin noticed the words were in her handwriting and felt a moment of pride—she had made this magic oil herself. Youth oil had been one of their biggest sellers, but more than likely this particular vial had been for Natacha's personal use. The witch had used a single drop in her diffuser every other night to turn back the gears of time and keep those wrinkles away.

Yasmin slipped the vial into her pocket. She already had three totems, but a backup couldn't hurt. She quickly repacked the box, poured the tea in the sink, and gathered up her items.

"Cheryl?" Yasmin asked, entering the living room. "Would it be okay if I borrowed a few things from that box?"

Cheryl didn't reply. Yasmin checked the dining room.

"Cheryl?"

She's probably on the phone or something, Yasmin thought, eyeing the front door. *You have what you came for. Just go. You still need to practice the incantation before tonight.*

Yasmin had her hand on the doorknob when she changed her mind. She couldn't leave without saying goodbye. Cheryl had welcomed her into her home. She had made her tea. True, it had been the most disgusting tea that Yasmin had ever tasted, but that hadn't been Cheryl's fault. There had been a sale.

"Cheryl?"

Yasmin walked down the short hallway that led to the bedrooms. Although the apartment looked different than when it had been magically augmented, the basic floor plan remained the same. Yasmin remembered the way.

"Cheryl?" she called again. The silence was unnerving. "Everything okay?"

The door to the master bedroom was slightly ajar. Yasmin gave it a single, hesitant knock. It swung open on squeaky hinges. The first thing Yasmin saw as more of the room was revealed were Cheryl's feet hanging over the left side of the bed. Next came her legs and torso. She was trembling slightly, as though having a bad dream.

The door continued to swing open. At last, all of Cheryl was revealed.

Yasmin bit back a scream.

A fleshy, translucent tube was covering the woman's mouth. It looked like some sort of worm. Cheryl screamed, the sound muffled by this grotesque mask, and shadowy, insectile shapes skittered out of her mouth. They crawled along the inside of the tube toward the opposite end, which lay beyond Yasmin's field of vision. She opened the door wider, following the pulsating tube, and nearly screamed herself when she saw its final destination: the ear of a figure standing a few feet from the bed.

Natacha.

Yasmin's heart thudded in her chest. *No! It can't be!*

Natacha's eyes were closed, but there was a satisfied smile on her face. As the shadowy insects crawled into her ear, she smacked her lips together like someone appreciating a good meal.

She was devouring Cheryl's fear.

Simeon didn't kill her, Yasmin realized. *He changed her into a nachpyr, like him.*

The feeding tube made a slurping sound as it detached itself from Cheryl's mouth and withdrew into Natacha's newly enlarged ear like a fishing line.

Natacha's eyes opened. They were now the same moon gray as Simeon's.

"Welcome back to my apartment, girl," she said.

Yasmin stumbled down the hallway and into the living room. Natacha followed. She wasn't wearing any makeup, and her skin was deathly pale.

"How do you like the new me?" Natacha asked, twirling around as if showing off a stylish dress. "I have to admit, Simeon surprised me there at the end. I really thought he was going to kill me, that little rascal! Fortunately, he only wanted to give Alex a scare to keep him in line. It was important for my terror to be as convincing as possible."

Natacha lunged forward, and Yasmin swung the ledger in a desperate attempt to defend herself. Laughing with delight, Natacha danced to the side and snatched the ledger away.

"What are you doing with *this*?" she asked, lovingly turning the book in her hands. She gazed with curiosity at the other items Yasmin was holding. "My hairbrush . . .

my old door number . . ." Her mouth curled into a devilish grin. "Are you trying to cast a spell? How precious! I was wondering why you were going to see Maria every day, but I never would have expected—oh, I can't wait to tell Simeon." Her voice grew sincere. "I'm glad I stopped you in time. Magic is dangerous stuff. You might end up wasting years of your life trying to be something you're not. I mean, not that you have years of your life left—more like minutes—but theoretically."

Natacha winced as a spine stinger emerged from the back of her neck. It was shorter than Simeon's but just as deadly looking.

"Thank you, by the way," Natacha said. "Without your help, I never would have discovered who I was truly meant to be. That's why I'm going to make your death quick, Yasmin. See! I remembered your name this time."

The spine stinger whipped toward Yasmin's neck. She jerked her head to the left, feeling the breeze of the telson as it whizzed past her and punched through the wall. Natacha tried to yank the stinger out for a second attack, but it was stuck, giving Yasmin a chance to scamper out of range.

She had bought herself a moment's grace, nothing more. What should she do? The front door was out. By the time she got it open, Natacha would be ready to attack again. Besides, Yasmin couldn't just abandon Cheryl.

She heard Alex's voice in her head.

Monsters always have a weak point. The stinger! Cut it off!

She needed a knife.

Yasmin dashed into the kitchen. Behind her, she heard a crumbling sound, a shriek of victory. *She's free*, Yasmin thought. She couldn't worry about that right now. She needed to find a weapon. There was a cutting board on the counter, but no knives—*seriously, Cheryl?*—so Yasmin frantically began to open one drawer after another. Silverware, place settings, *so* many boxes of tea . . . and then, at last, she struck gold: a massive butcher's knife with a heroically gleaming blade.

Yasmin reached for it, and the drawer slammed shut, nearly cutting off her fingers.

"What are you thinking?" Natacha whispered in her ear. "That's a grown-up knife! You could hurt yourself!"

Yasmin tried to run, but Natacha gripped her by the shoulders. The stinger swayed back and forth, tracking Yasmin's movements like an asp.

"If it makes you feel better," Natacha said, "we're not going to kill Alex. He's going to become one of us. Simeon considered giving that gift to you as well, but I talked him out of it. I knew you'd prefer it this way."

"You're right," Yasmin said.

In one fluid motion, she yanked the vial of essential

oil from her pocket, pulled out the stopper, and tossed the contents in Natacha's face.

"What is this?" Natacha screamed. She wiped the fluid from her face and sniffed her fingertips. "Beetle root. Clock essence. A touch of crushed nightberries. Is this youth oil?" Natacha clapped her hands against her cheeks. "Ahh! I'm going to look even prettier! The horror! The horror!"

In truth, Natacha's frown lines had smoothed out, and her skin, even without makeup, looked more lustrous than ever.

"No more messing around," she said, nodding toward the bedroom. "I left dinner on the table, and I don't want it to get cold."

Yasmin barely heard a word she said. Her attention was completely absorbed by the rapid changes taking place in Natacha's face. Just a moment ago, she had been a woman in her late twenties. Now, however, she could have passed for a high school student.

"Why are you looking at me like that?" Natacha asked. She checked her appearance in the nearest mirror. The effects of the oil seemed to be accelerating, because she was already younger than Yasmin and swimming in an older woman's clothes.

"You're only supposed to use a single drop at a time, diluted in three cups of water," Yasmin said. "Plus—that oil has been sitting there for a year now, and you know how beetle root works. It grows stronger the longer you let it age." Yasmin couldn't resist a tiny smile. "You're the one who taught me that."

Natacha—now an awkward-looking seven-year-old missing her two front teeth—shrieked in fury and charged at Yasmin. It was impossible to run while trapped in such oversized garments, however, and she fell almost immediately.

"No!" she screamed, slamming her fists on the floor. Natacha was shrinking rapidly now, vanishing beneath the folds of clothes. "I was finally me! I was finally—"

Her voice devolved into the cry of a baby. Soon even that stopped, and the bump beneath the clothing flattened out to nothing at all.

18

MOON STORY

Simeon was waiting for Alex the moment he appeared in the graveyard. The nachpyr was wearing a black suit with a red bow tie. His hair was combed neatly into place.

"Are you ready to be reborn?" he asked.

All Alex could manage was a hesitant nod. He supposed that was for the best. If he looked too eager, Simeon would know something was up.

"I've thought about it," Alex replied, "and maybe I am better suited to being a nachpyr. I mean, I already spend most of my time trying to scare people, so creating actual nightmares sounds like it would be right up my alley."

Simeon beamed with pleasure. "I'm glad you've finally seen reason. And you should know that you won't be alone. I've turned Natacha as well."

Alex put on his best look of surprise. He hoped it was

enough. Yasmin had risked calling him earlier to give him a heads-up on her eventful evening. The sound of her voice had brought tears to his eyes.

"I saw Natacha die!" Alex exclaimed. He thought about clapping a hand to his mouth, then decided that was over-doing it. "How's that possible?"

"There was a single drop of ichor on the tip of my stinger. That's all it takes for the change to take hold. To be honest, I was worried it wouldn't work anymore. Natacha is the first nachpyr I've made in a long, long time. I resented the thought of setting one of my kind loose in the world when I was still trapped in here. But now that my hibernation is finally drawing to a close, I want to make sure there are some servants waiting for me on the other side. I'm not going to be myself for the first few days. It takes a huge amount of strength to go from one world to the next. But we'll worry about that when the time comes." Simeon's spine stinger rose into the air. "This is going to leave a permanent scar, so I'll let you pick. Right side or left side?"

Although the stinger was within striking distance of his neck, Alex did his best to conceal his terror. He wanted Simeon to believe that he was truly looking forward to his metamorphosis. "Actually," Alex said, "if it's not too much trouble, I was hoping I could write a story first."

Simeon's eyes clouded with suspicion. "Why would you want to do that?"

"I don't *want* to, but I have this really good idea. Honestly, it might be the best idea I've ever had. I want to write it while it's fresh in my head."

"It's just one story," Simeon said with a pout. "There'll be plenty of other ones."

Alex took a moment to gather his courage. This next part was a huge gamble, but it was the only way to make Simeon believe him.

"You're right," Alex said. "It's too bad, though. This story is *so* dark and imaginative. It probably would have made an amazing cup of tea. Hopefully I'll still remember it later, but I can't make any promises. I tend to forget a lot of ideas." He laughed and waved a hand across the graveyard. "As you can see."

Simeon's expression grew pensive.

"You really think this flower will be special?" he asked.

"Positive. I thought it could be my gift to you to mark the occasion." He turned his neck to the left side, clearing a path for the stinger. "But whatever you think is best."

As Alex had hoped, his willingness to be turned seemed to put Simeon at ease.

"I suppose a few hours won't matter, if the prize is as good as you say. I'll wait right here." He gave Alex a playful nudge with his stinger. "Don't worry, my friend. You'll still be a nachpyr before this night is through."

Although Alex had indeed found what he was looking for in the bin of stories his mother had saved, he still wasn't convinced his theory was correct until he spotted the door in the painted moon. He was annoyed he hadn't noticed it earlier, though he supposed it was understandable; the door was the same shade of gray as the moon itself and nearly impossible to see unless you were looking for it. Alex tracked it across the graveyard, wondering how he was going to get up there. At last he bumped into a wooden backdrop painted like the night sky and climbed a series of rungs to his destination.

He opened the moon door and smiled at the sight before him.

Alex had often imagined what his office would look like if he ever became a real author when he grew up. This was it. In addition to a cozy couch and flat-screen TV with the latest video game console, the office was packed with horror memorabilia: a display case filled with dolls, shelves lined with creepy novels and short story collections, a ceramic Halloween village with working orange street-lights, gruesome movie posters, and a life-sized statue of Freddy Krueger (which Alex found pretty funny, under the circumstances). On the far side of the room was an ancient mahogany desk that looked like it had been stolen from Dracula's castle. The gravebook Alex needed was waiting for him. There was a tombstone on the cover. Alex checked the moon door and found a matching tombstone carved into the side facing the office.

It was further confirmation that his theory was correct.

Although he was tempted to keep exploring the office, Alex forced himself to take a seat at the desk instead. For his plan to work, he needed a story about a graveyard. And not just any story. It had to create a truly extraordinary flower.

Alex leaned back in the chair and closed his eyes, trying to think of a miraculous idea capable of accomplishing everything he needed.

Nothing came.

The pressure mounted within him.

Everything is riding on this story, he thought. *If I can't deliver, our plan is going to fail. Simeon will turn me into a monster. He'll punish Yasmin for what she did to Natacha.*

Alex had to come up with a good idea. No. Not a good idea. A perfect idea.

If I can't . . . If I can't . . .

But what if he could?

Alex took a deep breath and focused on the blank page before him. He was thinking too hard. It was just a story. He had written hundreds of them. He could do this.

Trust yourself, he thought. *Trust your talent.*

Just write.

It wasn't easy. It never was. But soon enough, Alex lost himself in the work. Words sprang from his pen and settled into their rightful place on the page. Before long, the story was done.

The gravebook burst into flames.

"Here goes nothing," Alex said, opening the moon door. The story graveyard stretched before him. From this height, he was able to see for miles in every direction, and the number of graves—no, *ideas*—filled him with pride. It really was a beautiful place.

"What are you *doing* up there?" Simeon shouted from below. He looked angry and bewildered. *Good,* Alex thought. If Simeon was confused, it meant he didn't understand what was about to happen.

Alex closed the moon door behind him and used the sky rungs to climb down to the graveyard.

"I'm done with my story," Alex said. "I was right, by the way. It's going to make a fantastic flower."

Simeon gave a distracted nod. His eyes remained on the painted moon.

"Why is that grave world so different than the others?" he asked.

"Because it's not a grave world." There was no turning back after this, so he decided to tell Simeon the truth.

Alex didn't have a particularly good reason for doing so. Mostly he just wanted to see the look on the nachpyr's face. "There's an office up there. Super cool. It's not an unfinished idea, though. It's just my regular old dream."

"Don't be ridiculous. This graveyard is your real dream."

Alex shook his head. "It took me forever to figure it out. Yasmin was the one who gave me the biggest clue, though I didn't realize it at the time. When she was waiting for me to finish one of my stories, she went exploring in the woods and found what we ended up calling a 'treadmill spot'—a place where you could keep walking forever and never move an inch."

Simeon gave a haughty shrug. "So what? Your idea was unfinished. There was only so far you could go."

"That's what we thought, too. But when you and Natacha abandoned me here that first time, I found a treadmill spot in the graveyard—more than one, actually. Which is weird, right? I mean, you'd expect that kind of thing in a tiny little idea, like you said, but this was supposed to be my real dream. It didn't mean much to me at the time, but later you told me, 'Even the simplest dream is an infinity of infinities.' Nice phrasing, by the way. It stuck with me. Eventually I started to wonder if this graveyard might not be a regular dream at all. What if it was just an unfinished story idea like the other ones?"

"Ludicrous," Simeon said, but Alex could see the doubt

beginning to form in his eyes.

"I searched through my old stories for anything involving graveyards. I found what I was looking for in my second-grade writing journal. 'The Weird Graveyard,' by Alex Mosher. Not much of a title, but I was eight, so cut me some slack. Here's the first line: 'At the end of a long dark road was a different kind of graveyard.' I didn't get much further than that, but I think you get it. I had an idea about a unique graveyard—or maybe a graveyard where something unique happened—and over the years, it grew and grew in my mind"—Alex held out his hands, encompassing everything around him—"until it became this."

"No," Simeon said, shaking his head. "It can't be."

Alex gave a bashful shrug. "Turns out my regular dream world is just a writing office. Not very impressive as far as dreams go, I guess, but it's pretty much heaven to me. I can read. I can write. What could be more 'infinity of infinities' than that? As for this place—you told me once that humans seek order, even in their dreams. Well, turns out I did the same thing. I tucked all my small ideas into one mega idea."

Simeon sneered. "Even if what you say is true, it changes nothing. I'm still going to turn you into a nachpyr. You will create all the flowers I want, for as long as I want. Speaking of which—where is this marvelous story you've written? How can this be a grave world when there's no gravestone?"

Alex smiled and pointed up at the sky. Words had begun to scroll across the moon, backlit by the silvery glow.

"You don't enter this particular idea through a grave," he said. "You enter it through a moon. Makes sense that's where the story would appear."

Simeon stared up at the moon, his cheeks flushed with anger and maybe, just maybe, a hint of fear. "You are still my prisoner, and you will do what I want—"

"Shh," Alex said, placing a finger to his lips. "I'm reading."

RING-RING

Meera Dhar opened her eyes. There was a bike in the driveway with a large red ribbon tied around the handlebars.

"Happy birthday!" Ms. Dhar exclaimed.

For a few moments, Meera was confused. This couldn't be her birthday present. The bike was pink, not the sleek black color she had wanted. Even worse—it was *used*. There must have been something in Meera's face that revealed her true feelings, because her mother's smile faltered. Meera immediately felt guilty and unappreciative.

"Thanks, Mom," she said, giving her a big hug. "I love it."

"No, you don't," said Ms. Dhar, brushing back Meera's hair. "But maybe you could learn to love it. I wish I could afford the new one you wanted, but this is probably as close as we're going to get. The man at the garage sale said his daughter took really good care of it. She loved this bike more than anything else in the world."

"Guess she got too big for it," Meera said.

Ms. Dhar paused before answering. "Lucky us, right?"

Meera nodded, taking a seat on the bike. She'd need to raise the saddle, and the white basket attached to the handlebars would have to go. Not only was it babyish, but the name ADDIE had been written in thick black marker across the wicker strips. Meera didn't need the entire world to know that she wasn't the bike's first owner.

At least the shiny silver bell on the handlebar was kind of cool. Meera pressed the thumb trigger.

Ring-ring. Ring-ring.

There was something unusual about the tone of the bell. It sounded almost sad. Or maybe that was just the way Meera felt right now.

"Well, don't just sit there," Ms. Dhar said. "Give it a whirl!"

Not wanting to make her mother feel bad, Meera pumped the pedals and shot down the driveway. This wasn't her dream bike, but the least she could do was give it a chance.

An hour later, Meera limped into the house, bruised and battered.

The bike was evil.

Sometimes it turned in the wrong direction or locked up completely and didn't turn at all. Sometimes the brakes didn't work. Sometimes the bike came to a screeching halt out of nowhere.

Meera told her mom the bike was broken.

"No way," Ms. Dhar said. "I gave it a full inspection before I let you ride it. The chain is lubed, the bolts tightened, the brakes oiled. The guy at the garage sale wasn't lying. His daughter treated that bike with love." Ms. Dhar kissed Meera on the forehead. "I think you're just a little out of practice, hon. It's been years since you've had a bike of your own."

Meera didn't argue. Her mom could fix anything, and if she said the bike was working fine, it was working fine. She parked the bike in the garage and promised herself she would give it another try tomorrow.

Ring-ring. Ring-ring.

Meera sat up in bed, groggy with sleep. Was that a dream, or had she just heard the bike bell? She listened carefully. The house was silent, until—

Ring-ring.

It wasn't a dream. Meera thought the sound was coming from the garage, which made sense. That was where she had left the bicycle. But who was ringing the bell? It couldn't be her mom. She was working the overnight shift at the hospital.

Meera was alone in the house.

Feeling the first inklings of fear, she got out of bed and walked barefoot to the garage. The automatic light was on the fritz again. In the darkness she heard:

Ring-ring. Ring-ring.

Meera's hand hovered over the light switch. She didn't want to turn it on. She wanted to lock the door and call her mom. Except what would she say? Please come home, the bike bell is ringing by itself? That was nonsense. There had to be a logical explanation. More than likely, the thumb trigger had gotten stuck. It was a used bike, remember? These things happened.

Gritting her teeth, Meera turned on the light.

Ms. Dhar took pride in a clean and orderly garage. Everything from tools to Meera's lacrosse equipment was in its proper spot. Except for the pink bike. It was supposed to be parked against the wall next to the gardening equipment. That was where Meera had left it.

Instead, the bike was at the front of the garage with its front tire pressed against the door. Meera's brain grasped at logical explanations and came up empty. The bike had moved. On its own. Just because it was impossible didn't make it any less true.

Ring-ring. Ring-ring.

Meera leaped back and slammed the door shut. She was tempted to run upstairs and lock herself in her room, but after a moment's consideration, something about the bell changed her mind. It was more than just sad. A word from an old vocabulary test rose into her head: *plaintive*. She opened the door to the garage again, just wide enough to take a peek. The bike was in the same position. Meera was reminded of a dog with its nose pressed against a patio door, begging to be let out. She hit the button that opened the garage door. For a full minute, the bike didn't move. And then, just as Meera was beginning to wonder if she was completely losing her mind, it drove off into the night.

Almost immediately, Meera heard a loud crash.

She took a cautious step forward and saw that the bike had fallen over at the end of the driveway. Its tires spun frantically, and the handlebars turned from left to right. There was something almost pathetic about the bike, like a bird with a broken wing.

Ring-ring. Ring-ring.

The bell didn't sound plaintive anymore. It sounded like a cry for help. Knowing she couldn't just leave it there, Meera righted the bike and quickly stepped back. The bike resumed its journey and got about ten feet before tipping over again.

Ring-ring, ring-ring.

This time, she held the handlebars in place until she was sure the bike had regained its balance. When she let go, it wobbled a few feet and would have crashed to the ground again if Meera hadn't caught it in time.

She heard a squeaking sound as the saddle rose a few inches.

"Are you . . . offering me a seat?"

Ring-ring.

Meera's curiosity nudged her fear out of the way. Why would the bike want her to sit down when it was perfectly capable of moving on its own? Unless . . .

"Do you need someone to ride you?" Meera asked. "Is that why you keep falling over?"

Ring-ring.

It was a bad idea to get on the bike. On the other hand, Meera felt like they had come to some sort of agreement, and she was curious. Where did this bike want to go so badly?

"If I help you, you won't hurt me. Right?"

Ring-ring.

Meera thought that sounded like a *yes*, though it could have easily been *I'm going to drive you straight off a bridge.* How could she know for sure? Meera didn't speak bike.

"Stay here," she said.

Meera ran back to the garage and put on all her lacrosse equipment—elbow and knee pads, chest protector, gloves—and her bicycle helmet. Now fully armored, she tossed a flashlight into the basket of the bike and took a seat.

The bike took off.

Unlike earlier that day, when they had been fighting for control, Meera let the bike take the lead. They rode for a long time. At last, they came to a screeching halt in front of a tall iron gate with a sign that read GLENVILLE CEMETERY.

"Seriously, bike?" Meera asked.

Ring-ring.

They had already come so far, however, and she didn't want to return home without any answers. After a long search, they found a hole in the fence big enough for both of them. There were no lights in the cemetery, but that didn't matter. The bike knew where it was going. After a few turns along the concrete paths, they slowed before a grave that looked newer than the others.

Meera got off the bike and used her flashlight to read the tombstone:

ADELAIDE THOMPSON

2013—2022

Sleep, my little one, sleep.

It didn't take long for Meera to make the connection. She shone her flashlight on the white basket to make sure she remembered the name correctly. ADDIE appeared in a halo of light.

"Was she your owner?" Meera asked the bike.

Ring-ring.

"Do you miss her?"

Ring-ring. Ring-ring.

Meera's eyes grew teary. The bike wasn't scary. It was sweet and tender and loyal.

"I understand if you want to stay," Meera said. "But if you want to come home with me, that's okay, too. I know we're not each other's first choice. But maybe we could learn to be each other's second choice."

Ring-ring.

The tone was both plaintive and final. This time, Meera was positive she understood what the bike was trying to say.

Goodbye.

"All right, then," Meera said, patting its saddle. "Goodbye, bike."

She started back along the path. It was a long way home from here, but Meera thought she knew the way.

Ring-ring. Ring-ring.

She turned around. The bike was wobbling in her direction. It came to an unsteady halt in front of her. *It was saying good-bye to Addie, not me!* Meera realized with a jolt of happiness. That was the reason they had come here. One last goodbye before a new life could begin.

"Let's go home," Meera said.

Ring-ring.

They rode off. By the time they reached the street, the bike even let Meera drive.

Simeon scowled at the words emblazoned across the moon. "The bike and the girl became *friends*? How is that scary?"

"It wasn't meant to be," Alex said. "I wanted to try something different. Stretch my imagination."

Simeon scoffed. "Then where's the flower?"

Alex didn't have a good answer for that. He had been wondering the same thing himself, and it was starting to make him nervous.

"Enough of this nonsense," Simeon said. "Let's get down to business. Once you're a nachpyr, you'll never write a happy ending again."

Simeon strode forward. Alex could tell there would be no stopping him this time. The nachpyr raised his spine stinger into a striking position and Alex saw a drop of ichor dangling from the tip, more than enough to change a terrified boy into a soulless fear vampire.

He covered his neck with his hands and braced himself.

"What's that?" Simeon asked.

A pink flower was descending between them like a miniature hot-air balloon. It was unlike any flower Alex had ever seen. A dozen petals enclosed inside a larger circle spun like the spokes of a wheel, making a melodic clicking noise. The flower was beautiful because it was strange, and strange because it was beautiful.

Simeon pressed it to his nose.

"This fragrance is *sublime!*" he exclaimed. "With tea this potent, I'll be back to my old self in no time at all."

He closed his eyes and took another long whiff of the flower. Alex used this opportunity to withdraw the strand of hair from his pocket and place it on the back of Simeon's head.

It wiggled deep and took root like a vine.

"Grow," Alex said.

The effect was instantaneous. Blond hair shot out in all directions, anchoring itself deep in the ground and lassoing around tombstones and tree limbs. The nachpyr screamed in fury and tried to charge Alex, but the hair held him in check.

"What is *this*?" he hissed.

"A present from a friend," Alex said. In all the commotion, the bicycle flower had fallen from Simeon's hand; Alex quickly placed it in the pouch Lenore had brought him. "Turns out Natacha isn't the only witch in town. This pouch is magic, too. Anything I put in here can make the trip back with me to the waking world."

"That flower is *mine*."

"Come and get it, then."

Simeon laughed. "You think this pathetic trap will stop me? You obviously know nothing about dream walkers." He snapped his fingers, no doubt intending to hop into another dream. When nothing happened, his face grew panicked. "Why can't I leave? What have you done to me?"

"The same thing you did to Lenore. Hurts, doesn't it."

"What do you *want*?"

"For starters, I want to wake up."

"Absolutely not. You're staying here with me. Eventually I'll get out of this trap, and then I'm going to make you wish you were never born."

The ground began to rumble.

"You forgot something," Alex said. "This is a grave world, and I've just finished a story. You know what happens next."

For the first time, Alex saw genuine fear in Simeon's eyes.

"Let me go," he said, "and I'll leave you alone. I promise. It'll be like none of this ever happened."

"But it did happen. There's nothing you can do to change that."

Tombstones began to shoot off like rockets. They vanished into the moon, which had transformed into a gaping maw.

"You win," the nachpyr said with a sneer. "I'll return to the waking world. But I'm going to leave you right here. My only regret is I won't be able to see this world swallow you whole."

"You could do that," Alex said, shouting to be heard over the wailing wind. He raised the pouch. "But look at what you'd be leaving behind. You don't want this precious imagination to be destroyed, do you? The only way to save it is to wake me up. Do that, and the pouch comes back with me. I'll give it to you in the real world, as long as you promise to let me go after that."

Simeon struggled against his hairy manacles. His pitiless eyes were a different kind of void than the one above him.

"Let's not lie to each other, Alex. You're well aware that I will never let you go. I'm going to take that flower. After that . . . I feel a little of the old imagination stirring. I'm sure I'll think of something."

A willow tree was torn from the ground and eaten by the hungry moon. Its dangly roots waved goodbye.

"Awake," snarled Simeon.

19

THE SPELL

Yasmin sat on the aluminum bleachers and waited for Alex to arrive. The park, so full of life and laughter during the daylight hours, felt ominous at night. She wondered if she had made a mistake choosing this place.

Too late now, she thought.

At last, Yasmin saw a familiar figure running across the grass. She ran to meet him.

They hugged for a long time.

"I was so worried about you," Yasmin said.

"I was worried about me, too," Alex replied. "But I think everything is going to be okay now."

"How do you know?"

Alex looked down at his feet. "Because you're here."

Yasmin smacked him in the shoulder. Hard.

"Ow!" he exclaimed. "What was that for?"

"You're going to make me cry, and we don't have time for that. Wait—where's Lenore?"

"She's still recovering from bringing me your message. That growth where her tail used to be has gotten so heavy it's like dragging an anchor behind her. I couldn't ask her to walk all this way." His lower lip began to tremble. "She sleeps most of the day now, and I think she's in a lot of pain. Lenore is a witch's familiar. She's meant to be magic. I'm not sure she can live without her tail."

Yasmin felt a knot in her stomach. She had been so worried about saving Alex that she hadn't really noticed Lenore was in such bad shape. Or maybe Lenore, brave little soldier that she was, had done her best to hide it.

"We'll bring her to Ms. Goffel tomorrow," Yasmin said. "She'll know what to do."

"I don't know. We don't have the best track record with witches."

"Ms. Goffel is different. We can trust her. Think about how much she's helped us tonight! And all she asked for in return is for you to read her a story."

Alex's mouth dropped open. "And you said *yes*?"

"You're just paranoid because every time someone wants your stories, they end up trying to kill you."

"Exactly!" Alex shook his head and scanned the park. "We'll sort this out later. Any sign of Simeon?"

"Not yet. You sure he'll be able to find us?"

Alex nodded and opened his backpack. It contained Ms. Goffel's leather pouch, two flashlights, and a copy of a book called *We Have Always Lived in the Castle.* Yasmin picked it up and gave Alex a questioning look. He shrugged.

"In case it's a long wait," he said. "Why'd you pick the park, anyway? It's creepy at night."

"Ms. Goffel said I should choose a place where I felt comfortable and confident. That would make it easier to cast the spell, like a home-field advantage."

Alex stared at the baseball field. "I hope you didn't take her too literally." He opened the pouch and carefully withdrew a strange orange flower that instantly began to spin in the wind like a pinwheel. The air was filled with a tantalizing fragrance that made Yasmin think of running out of school into the open arms of summer.

"It's beautiful," she said.

"Thank you," Alex replied, beaming with pride. "Where should I put it?"

As Yasmin led Alex to the infield, she told him all about the totems. It was dark, though not so dark that they needed the flashlights.

"I can't believe you went back to the apartment," Alex said. "That was so brave."

"No one is more surprised than me," Yasmin said with a laugh. "I may even go back again. The woman who lives there now is super cool, and I feel like I owe her an explanation since she almost died because of me." She pointed out the totems. "Hairbrush on third base. Natacha's ledger on second. The old '4E' on first. See how the objects form a triangle? We want Simeon inside of it—so I'd put the flower midway between second and the mound. That's about dead center."

"Got it. The flower is like bait."

"Not 'like' bait. It *is* bait. Sometimes you get a little simile happy. Have I ever told you that?"

Alex rolled his eyes. "Everyone's a critic."

With the flower and totems in place, all they could do was wait. They hid beneath the bleachers. Yasmin kept an eye on the field while Alex watched the street, just in case Simeon came from that direction. Occasionally, Yasmin used the flashlight to review the incantation Ms. Goffel had written for her. The pronunciations were tricky, and although Yasmin had practiced them over and over again, she was worried she might stumble in the heat of the moment. Alex practiced with her, and the words came so easily to him that Yasmin wondered if he might be a better choice to cast the spell. After all, Alex had also been imprisoned in the apartment. The totems would work for him as well as her.

No, she thought. *You need to do this.*

It was a warm night, but Yasmin still wished she had

worn something heavier than just jeans and a T-shirt. Then again, maybe it wouldn't have helped. The chill that pierced her bones had nothing to do with the temperature.

"What if he doesn't show?" Yasmin whispered.

"He'll be here," Alex said. "He's too weak to go back into the dream world, but he's also not ready to feed again. He needs that flower to survive. Besides, he really hates us."

"The feeling's mutual."

The night marched on. At last, Yasmin caught movement in the distance. She nudged Alex—who had actually fallen asleep—and together they watched a dark shape cross the outfield grass. As Simeon came into the light, Yasmin bit back a scream. Perhaps moving from the dream world to the waking world was a complicated business that involved taking a body apart and putting it back together again. Perhaps Simeon had simply been in a rush, anxious to escape the world falling to pieces around him. For whatever reason, things hadn't gone according to plan. Simeon's neck now ended in a perfect stump, and his head had been relocated to the end of his stinger spine, where it rose and fell like a grotesque cobra. Gone was his boyish appearance; the nachpyr's horrifying, ancient face looked like the result of an immortality potion gone awry.

"Alex," Simeon said. His eyes reflected the light of the unpainted moon. "Yasmin. I know you're both out there. I can smell your fear."

Simeon stepped onto the infield, his bare feet making crunching sounds in the dirt. Yasmin began reading the incantation, keeping her voice low so the nachpyr couldn't hear her. If all went well, he wouldn't know she was casting the spell until it was too late.

"Ahh," Simeon said as he spotted the flower. His stinger spine lowered his head to the ground. As he inhaled the flower's sweet fragrance, his mouth creaked open in a smile, revealing blackened gums and a noticeable lack of teeth. Alex supposed it didn't matter. He wasn't that type of vampire.

Simeon extended his head in their direction, searching the darkness.

"This is obviously a trap," he said. "You're as subtle in real life as you are in your stories, Alex. Hmm . . . so, the flower is meant to be a distraction, but from what? If this was back in my glory days, I'd expect villagers with torches and pitchforks. But that time has passed, so what could it be?"

Yasmin finished her first pass of the incantation, and semitransparent walls suddenly appeared, linking the three totems. These weren't just any walls, however. Yasmin recognized the red wallpaper with black flowers.

"It's the apartment!" Alex exclaimed in wonder. "The spell's working!"

Yasmin began reading the incantation a second time. *You can do this*, she thought. Despite this renewed confidence, however, she noticed that the words were harder to say. The spell was pulling from some source of energy she didn't even know she had, and it was already beginning to empty.

Simeon laughed, sending a chill along Yasmin's spine.

"Oh—your plan is just magic," he said. "For a moment there, I was actually worried."

Alex and Yasmin came out into the open; there was no longer any reason to hide. Yasmin continued to read, using the light of the walls for illumination. Apartment 4E was beginning to re-create itself. The bookcase full of magical objects. The antique furniture. The chair where Alex once sat to read his stories.

"You're almost there!" Alex exclaimed.

As Yasmin began the incantation a third time, her nose started to bleed. She wiped it with her sleeve and kept reading.

"You've done surprisingly well," Simeon said. "Honorably, even. But when you get right down to it, a spell is only as strong as the witch casting it, which is usually a matter of experience. Correct me if I'm wrong, but this is your first spell ever, isn't it?"

The words began to swim in front of Yasmin, causing her to mess up one of the more difficult phrases. A sofa and half the bookcase vanished.

"I thought so," Simeon said.

He calmly placed his palms against the magical wall and began pushing it in their direction. As he moved forward—the wall stretching to allow his progress—Yasmin felt the air being squeezed from her lungs. She stopped reading. The furniture and other details vanished. Soon it was only the walls. Holes began to appear in them, like taffy that had been stretched too far.

Simeon took a fourth step. A fifth.

Yasmin managed a single word, her face damp with sweat. It didn't do any good. Soon the wall would collapse. When that happened, there would be no way to stop Simeon. It was too much to ask. She couldn't do this alone.

You don't have to, she thought.

"Alex," she croaked, holding the incantation out to him. "Together. This will only work . . . together."

Alex added his voice to hers. In no time at all, they had found their rhythm; they were best friends, and the groundwork had already been laid. Their voices rose into the night—one voice, really—and the walls repaired themselves and returned to their previous strength, knocking Simeon backward.

The apartment began to refurnish itself at astonishing speed.

Simeon banged against the walls with all his might, but

they would no longer budge. Finally, he gave up. "Fine," he snapped. "You've trapped me. So what? You can't keep me here forever."

"No," said a voice behind him. "They can't."

Simeon turned to face Natacha. This wasn't the magic thief or the monstrous nachpyr. This was the version of Natacha from Yasmin's nightmares. She was tall and regal, like a fairy-tale queen from a lost story. Her inky eyes were swollen with dark magic.

Natacha had become a real witch at last.

She cackled with delight and raised her hands into the air. Black lightning danced between them before striking Simeon with such terrifying force that his hastily assembled body broke apart like a cheap doll. The legs went one way. The spine stinger another. The head rolled across the dirt and came to a stop directly across from Yasmin and Alex. Simeon's gray eyes fastened on the children who had bested him.

The nachpyr managed a final scream of rage and then was silent forever.

20

INTRODUCTIONS AND CONCLUSIONS

Three weeks later, they finally made their way to Snip, Snap, Snout. Ms. Goffel clapped her hands with glee and shooed her current customer out of the barber's chair. The man looked normal enough, but when Alex glanced in the mirror, he caught a glimpse of a shambling corpse.

"I brought you coffee," Yasmin said, placing a paper cup on the counter. "Sugar and a splash of cream, just the way you like it."

"You're the bee's knees, Yasmin," Ms. Goffel said. It was hard for Alex to imagine she was a famous witch; with her long gray braid and welcoming smile, she looked like she should be selling organic produce at a farmers' market. "And you must be the famous Alex Mosher, storyteller extraordinaire. I've heard so much about you."

"Yasmin has told me all about you, too," he said,

returning her pouch. "Thanks for your help. If it hadn't been for you—"

"It was nothing. After everything you've been through, you kids deserved a little help." Ms. Goffel placed her bone-handled shears on the counter so she could take a sip of coffee. "Where's that adorable cat of yours? I thought I was going to take a look at her tail. Familiars have amazing healing powers, so I was hoping it would grow back on its own—that's why I didn't offer to help earlier. But if it's still ailing her . . ."

Yasmin let out a long sigh. "Things have taken a turn. We were afraid to move her."

"I'm sorry to hear that. But maybe it's not as bad as you think. Sometimes things need to get worse before they get better."

Ms. Goffel's next customer started banging on the back door.

"Hold your horses!" she screamed. "Take a seat, Alex. That's the only thing that will shut them up. Besides, you could use a haircut."

"Later," Alex said, climbing into the chair. "I owe you a story first. I wrote a special one just for the occasion. I figured it was the least I could do."

Ms. Goffel held a hand to her heart. "A story just for me? Aren't you the sweetest thing!"

Alex pulled out his latest nightbook. The front and

back covers were blanketed with pictures. In addition to the usual assortment of creepy images, there were a few photos of Alex's family and a recent shot of Alex and Yasmin at Citi Field.

He started to read.

THE TENT OF BROKEN DOLLS

It was the first time a carnival had ever visited our nothing little town, so my best friend Liam and I couldn't wait to check it out. We were there when they first opened on Friday night, shoving our entry fees into the hand of the grizzled old cashier—a crisp five for me, crumpled ones and a handful of coins for Liam— and sprinting with mad joy across the grass. The carnival spoke the language of our boyish hearts: the screams of spinning riders, the calliope music from the carousel, the carnival barker promising HORRORS and WONDERS beyond our imagination. After gorging ourselves on funnel cake and fresh-squeezed lemonade, we followed the barker's siren call to a quieter part of the carnival beyond the lights and sounds.

A single black tent sat in the middle of the grassy field.

In front of the closed flaps was a girl dressed like a doll with a wig of red yarn hair and big blush circles on her cheeks. Even so, she was the kind of pretty that was beyond debate, and it was hard to look away from her without wanting to immediately look back again.

"Are you here to see the broken dolls?" she asked.

Liam and I exchanged an uneasy look and nodded.

"Excellent," the girl exclaimed, removing a tiny pouch. "The dolls require a small donation before you enter the tent. Button, shoelace, or hair. Any of them will help, but we're running low on buttons, so if it's all the same to . . ."

Ms. Goffel burst into tears. Alex looked down at his nightbook, confused.

"I haven't gotten to the sad part yet," he said.

"It's not the story," Ms. Goffel said between loud sobs. "I just feel so *bad*. Yasmin, I've been using you since the beginning. I was so mad at you! You killed Natacha!"

Yasmin swallowed nervously. "So you lied to me. You and Natacha *were* friends."

"Ugh—no. She was a horrid woman. But after she died, I couldn't get my magic oils anymore, which was one of my very few pleasures. I never thought I'd have a chance to take my revenge, but then you just showed up out of the blue, and I thought, 'Maria. This is a sign.' It wasn't just you I wanted, though. I wanted the storyteller, too. My original plan was to help you free Alex and then lure him here so I could cut his hair with the bone shears . . . the ones that can never be used on living people . . . oh, it's just horrible to think about what might have happened!"

"What stopped you?" Yasmin asked.

"I started to look forward to your visits way more than any magic oil." She sighed and looked down at her feet. "But I guess that's over now. I imagine you'll never come back here again, and I can't say I blame you."

Yasmin gave Ms. Goffel a hug.

"Sorry, but you're not getting rid of us that easily," she

said. "I was even thinking of getting bangs."

Ms. Goffel's expression grew hopeful. "You think you could really trust me after this?"

"We never doubted you for a minute," Yasmin said. "Right, Alex?"

"Absolutely," Alex said, looking past Ms. Goffel to where Lenore sat on the counter with the bone shears in her tiny hands, ready to clip off the witch's braid if necessary. Ms. Goffel had been correct—witches' familiars really did have excellent healing powers, and just a few days after their final encounter with Simeon, the shell that Lenore had been dragging around finally cracked open, revealing a brand-new tail. It was black with orange stars, and judging from the hours Lenore had spent preening in the mirror, she was thrilled with her new look. The kids had decided that it would be in their best interest to have Lenore on standby, just in case Ms. Goffel got any funny ideas.

Alex gave Lenore a nod, and the cat placed the bone shears back on the counter. She vanished just before Ms. Goffel turned in her direction. There was no need for the witch to know how close they had come to seeing what her special shears did to the living.

"Would you like to hear the rest of the story?" Alex asked.

"I'd love that," Ms. Goffel said.

"Me too," added Yasmin.

They returned to the world of broken dolls. It was one of Alex's longest tales. There was terror, betrayal, monsters, heroes, heartache, and—when all seemed lost—a happy ending. It was that last part that made it all worthwhile.

ACKNOWLEDGMENTS

I have been far more fortunate than poor Alex; the people who ask me to write stories are always unfailingly kind and supportive, and hardly ever try to lock me in magic apartments or dream realms.

As with *Nightbooks*, my editor, Katherine Tegen, played an integral part in shaping this book into the much improved version you currently hold in your hands. In addition, I am very grateful to the rest of the team at KT Books, including—but not limited to—Sara Schonfeld, Amy Ryan, Shona McCarthy, Mark Rifkin, Megan Gendell, Emily Mannon, and Aubrey Churchward.

Thank you, Dan Burgess, for another stunning book cover!

My agents are a dream team who deserve a ton of credit for all the good things that have happened in my career: Alexandra Machinist, who has been there from the start, Josie Freedman (the guiding force behind the Netflix adaptation of *Nightbooks*), and the marvelous Roxane Edouard, who has helped my stories reach kids all over the world. Shout-out as well to Romel Adam, Mason Novick, Sam Raimi, and the cast and crew of the *Nightbooks* movie. Thanks for making my dream come true.

Of course, none of this would be possible without the love and support of my family: Yeeshing, Jack, Logan, and Colin. Thanks for letting Alex borrow me all those long weekends.

And finally, thank you to all the readers who loved *Nightbooks* and begged for a sequel. This book wouldn't exist without you.

SPOOKY BOOKS *by* J. A. WHITE

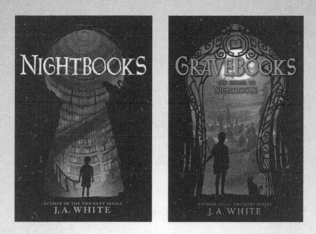

"A thrilling tale of magic that is just scary enough."
—*KIRKUS REVIEWS*

SHADOW SCHOOL

"The suspense is engaging and consistent throughout, and there's a perfect mix of scares and mystery that will entice even the most fainthearted of readers."
—*SCHOOL LIBRARY JOURNAL*

 KATHERINE TEGEN BOOKS
An Imprint of HarperCollins Publishers

harpercollinschildrens.com

GET CAUGHT UP IN
THE THICKETY

BOOK 1

BOOK 2

BOOK 3

BOOK 4

Read them all!

★ "Absolutely thrilling."—*PublishersWeekly* (starred review)

★ "Spellbinding."—*Kirkus Reviews* (starred review)

KATHERINE TEGEN BOOKS
An Imprint of HarperCollins Publishers

harpercollinschildrens.com